"Come here," he said quietly.

She rested her head on his shoulder with a sigh. Gently he pressed his cheek against her hair and with slow, easy movements massaged her shoulders.

For a long time they sat there without speaking, the swing rocking back and forth in the cool evening.

As she relaxed against him, he decided, finally, that everything had been worth it. If it had been necessary to undergo the struggles and dark years to reach this moment with Maggie, he would gladly endure them all again.

She trusted him.

Suddenly that knowledge gave him a knife thrust of sorrow, for eventually he would have to betray that trust. His chest tightened with guilt. Oh, Maggie, Maggie, he thought, I hope you'll find a way to forgive me when the time comes.

It was wrong, he could see that now. But as he held her in his arms, he didn't see how he could give up—not yet . . .

Dear Reader,

Welcome to the Silhouette **Special Edition** experience! With your search for consistently satisfying reading in mind, every month the authors and editors of Silhouette **Special Edition** aim to offer you a stimulating blend of deep emotions and high romance.

The name Silhouette **Special Edition** and the distinctive arch on the cover represent a commitment—a commitment to bring you six sensitive, substantial novels each month. In the pages of a Silhouette **Special Edition**, compelling true-to-life characters face riveting emotional issues—and come out winners. Both celebrated authors and newcomers to the series strive for depth and dimension, vividness and warmth, in writing these stories of living and loving in today's world.

The result, we hope, is romance you can believe in. Deeply emotional, richly romantic, infinitely rewarding—that's the Silhouette **Special Edition** experience. Come share it with us—six times a month!

From all the authors and editors of Silhouette **Special Edition**,

Best wishes,

Leslie Kazanjian,
Senior Editor

RUTH WIND

Summer's Freedom

Silhouette Special Edition

Published by Silhouette Books New York

America's Publisher of Contemporary Romance

For Denise West,
who loves and endures no matter what

SILHOUETTE BOOKS
300 East 42nd St., New York, N.Y. 10017

ISBN: 0-373-09588-0

First Silhouette Books printing March 1990

Books by Ruth Wind

Silhouette Special Edition

Strangers on a Train #555
Summer's Freedom #588

RUTH WIND

has been addicted to books and stories for as long as she can remember. When she realized at the age of seven that some lucky people actually spent their days spinning tales for others, she knew she had found her calling. The direction of that calling was decided when the incurable romantic fell in love with the films *Dr. Zhivago* and *Romeo and Juliet*.

The Colorado native holds a bachelor's degree in journalism and lives with her husband and two young sons in a town at the foot of the Rockies.

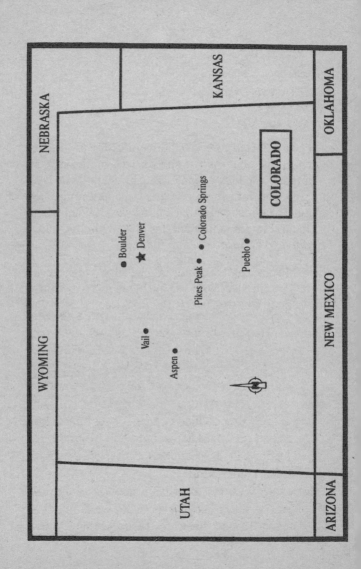

Prologue

September

He stepped into the bright, hot day with a sense of numbness, looking first to the mountains, dark blue on the horizon, then to the sky, a clear turquoise painted with streaks of feathery white. A wind, warm and scented with pine, danced over open fields to brush his face with light, playful buffets.

On his body were civilian clothes—jeans and a clean cotton shirt. His sister had brought him his boots and a good leather belt. His hair, freshly cut, lifted over his forehead in the free wind.

For a long moment, he simply stood at the threshold of his new life, unable to quite believe all that had happened in the past week. As he stood there, a butterfly flittered through the air—bright yellow with spots of blue.

His numbness burst, like the chrysalis that had once held the butterfly, and from the deadness surged a thrust of pure joy. He turned to the man next to him and grinned.

"You never did belong here," his friend said. "Go on, now. Don't look back. Remember what happened to Lot's wife."

"Thanks," he said simply, and took the first long steps into a future he'd never dreamed he would own.

Chapter One

By the time Maggie Henderson and her photographer arrived at the scene of the protest late Wednesday afternoon, a crowd had gathered. Maggie glanced at the heavy clouds hanging low over Cheyenne Mountain and turned to her photographer. "Rain would be the best thing that could happen this afternoon," she said.

"I'll second that," Sharon McConnell agreed, tossing one of a plethora of braids out of her eye.

"Come on," Maggie said as she pushed through a throng of black-leather-jacketed teens toward the center of the demonstration.

In front of a record store, a handful of teenagers dressed in pressed skirts and slacks marched in a slow circle, carrying placards protesting a rock band. From somewhere in the crowd, a portable radio blasted the music of the band, adding to the general chaos of shouts and chants.

Maggie couldn't take notes in the jostling crowd, so she committed it all to memory—the noise and taunts and clashing cultures of the two groups. Suddenly, the crowd parted a fraction and Maggie caught sight of a slender, blond girl seated on the hood of a car. She looked a little scared, Maggie thought, in spite of her black jacket studded with metal and swinging skull earrings.

Maggie grabbed Sharon's arm. Shouting to be heard, she said, "Get as much as you can. I've got to go kill my daughter."

Sharon's dark eyes widened in sympathy as she nodded. Maggie headed through the crowd toward Samantha, unintentionally pushing in her haste to get to the fifteen-year-old trying so hard to be grown-up. These kids were all at least a year or two older than Sam, Maggie fumed. She had no idea what she was getting into.

"Hey, watch it, lady," protested a girl in a striped tube top.

Maggie ignored her. The chants and noise were growing louder, and a kind of rocking motion rippled through the mass of teenagers. Distantly she heard the sound of sirens. Maggie caught a glimpse of Samantha jumping down from the hood of the car, before the crowd shifted again. Maggie was flung against the body of a boy, who shoved her roughly back. She staggered. The unmistakable sound of shattering glass sent a split second of silence over the crowd.

Then all hell broke loose.

As the bodies around her surged and pushed and roared, Maggie looked desperately for Samantha. She could see nothing but the black-and-silver jackets, jeans and flying hair. Someone screamed. The sirens arrived at the scene.

Maggie ducked flying fists, moving back as far as she could, intent now on saving herself from the unparalleled rage of teens who believed themselves wronged. A whisper of cool air touched her face, indicating a break in the hot press of bodies. She turned to flee.

An elbow, a knee, a fist—something unmoving and hard smashed into her left temple. Maggie staggered backward, clutching automatically at her head. She blinked hard and tried to stay on her feet.

The reporter in her knew that falling under the running crowd would be instant death. In spite of the stars shining with silver light in her eyes, she knew she had to keep her wits in whatever shape she could manage.

It wasn't much. She stumbled, carried along in the flow of the crowd, and collapsed on the curb, blood streaming into her eye. Head wounds bleed a lot, she told herself, praying she wouldn't need stitches.

"Maggie!" Sharon knelt next to her.

"Am I gonna make deadline?" Maggie asked weakly.

"Forget deadline—can you stand up?"

"I think so." With Sharon's help, she made it to her feet, pressing her palm hard to the wound. "I'm going to strangle a certain young woman as soon as I get home."

"You won't have to wait," said a soft, contrite voice at her side.

Maggie reached out and grabbed Samantha to her. One of the skull earrings bit into her jaw, and she smelled the strawberry scent of Sam's shampoo. Relief flooded through her.

"Come on," Sharon said. "Let's get you to the hospital."

Later, as she held a fresh ice pack to the wound marring her eyebrow, Maggie thought the entire afternoon would make a wonderful letter to her brother, Galen, in New Mexico. He would love the absurdity of the three dozen calls she'd made to the newsroom of the small weekly newspaper she owned and edited, frantically trying to make sure that the paper would get to the printer in time for distribution tomorrow afternoon. He would laugh at her descriptions of the lecture Samantha had received about the dangers of not exercising proper judgment in the selection of companions, a speech Maggie had delivered with an ice pack pressed to her blackening eye.

She swallowed a mouthful of cold beer and kicked the front porch swing into a little rocking motion. The May night was incredibly warm for a Colorado spring. Maggie breathed in the gentle breeze, fragrant with the odor of new grass, and felt its recuperative powers spread through her shoulders and down her spine.

Samantha, looking a great deal more like herself in a ponytail and a pink cotton sweat suit, appeared at the screen door. "Do you need anything, Mom? I'm about to go to bed."

"'Mom'?" Maggie echoed. "You've been calling me Maggie for weeks."

Sam had the grace to look ashamed. "I know. I'm sorry. But you really are my only mother, aren't you?"

"You know I am. I'll see you in the morning, okay?"

"Good night."

"'Night, Sam," Maggie answered gently.

She took another long swallow of beer. Sam would be sixteen soon. At the end of her first year in high school, she was beginning to ask difficult questions of herself, Maggie and the world around her—a normal, healthy step, but one complicated in Sam's case by a search for identity.

Given the girl's tangled parentage, the search was no surprise.

Sam's mother, a photographer, had been killed in a bomb blast in Belfast when Samantha was nearly four. Maggie had met and married Paul Henderson, also a photographer, when Sam was five, becoming the only mother Sam had really known. Five years later, an amicable but imperative divorce had split Maggie and Paul. Since Paul traveled widely in his career, the decision that Samantha would live with Maggie had been a sensible one.

For the most part, the arrangement had worked out well. Even Sam's present search for roots was not unexpected.

From the open door of the other half of the semi-detached building came the sound of quiet blues. Maggie swung slowly in time to the sound of the mournful saxophone. At least her new neighbor wasn't like the last ones, she thought, two single girls who had played their music until two or three in the morning, entertained friends constantly and even sunbathed in the backyard with their boom-box at full blast. Although she had liked the girls, their noise had become a serious problem. Maggie hadn't been sorry when they'd moved the week before.

Judging from the clues she'd gathered about the new neighbor, it was a man. Few women drove a truck or moved in during the course of one afternoon without the help of friends.

Now she added another tidbit of information—someone quiet, with a taste for blues. Nice.

As if on cue, a shadow emerged from the door of the other apartment. He walked out to his side of the porch and leaned on the railing. When Maggie's swing squeaked, he turned, almost imperceptibly crouching as if to spring.

Seeing her, he straightened. "Sorry," he said in a voice as deep as a mountain gorge. "I thought you'd gone in."

He was huge; four or five inches past six feet, with arms like the branches of a great tree. "That's all right," Maggie said. "It's your porch, too."

He relaxed on the sturdy wooden railing of the turn-of-the-century porch. "Thanks." His face was in shadow, but Maggie instinctively warmed to the gentleness of his resonant bass voice. "I didn't want to bother you."

"No, not at all," Maggie answered lazily. "There's nothing quite as relaxing as a spring night, is there?"

"I can't think of anything," he agreed. After a moment, he asked, "Is that a black eye you're nursing?"

Maggie lowered the ice pack, nodding ruefully. "I'll probably look like a boxer by morning. Seven stitches right through the eyebrow."

He made a sympathetic noise. "Bet that hurts."

"It's all right now, I think."

"Did you run into a wall?"

"Yes," Maggie said with a laugh. "A wall of teenagers."

"Teenagers?" He sounded perplexed.

"I run a small newspaper directed toward thirteen through seventeen-year-olds," she explained. "We cover all the news of their community—and unfortunately, the news of the moment is a series of confrontations about a rock band. I got caught in the middle this afternoon."

He stood to face her, leaning on the support post. "So then you're Maggie Henderson, right? Of the *Wanderer*?"

"That's me," she said, surprised. Not many people over the age of twenty had much use for the paper. "You've read it?"

"Yes. I like the music reviews."

"Thanks. I'll pass that on to the assistant editor, who's also my photographer." Maggie gave a small laugh. "And tonight she's doing everything, since I'm incapacitated."

"Talented woman."

"Yes."

"The paper is a great idea—most people overlook teenagers."

"I agree. I don't think it's ever been tougher to be that age." Odd, Maggie thought. Perhaps it was the darkness or her exhaustion or his gentle, vibrant voice, but she felt utterly comfortable with this stranger, even in her oversize T-shirt and worn-out jeans. "How do you like your new house?" she asked.

"I love all the windows," he said, "and the bookshelves in the living room. Are both sides exactly alike?"

Maggie sipped a bit of her beer and let its golden chill cool her throat before she answered. "There's a breakfast nook on your side that we don't have, but that's the only difference."

"You can't find places like this too often anymore," he said. "Everybody's building condos and putting in microwaves."

"Speaking of microwaves," Maggie said with a laugh, "don't ever run too many appliances at once. My coffee maker in combination with the microwave or even the VCR kicks off the breakers."

He chuckled appreciatively. "I'll remember that. I just bought a microwave." A pause, somehow filled

with the lingering sound of his laughter, fell. "I don't
know how to use it, yet, but I guess I'm going to
learn," he added after a moment, a hint of self-
deprecation in his tone.

"Don't worry. I was terrified of mine at first, but it
seemed almost criminal not to have one as fast as they
cook things. My daughter's the one who figured it all
out for me."

"Really?"

"She can use it to cook anything now." Now that's
a bit of scintillating conversation, Maggie, she
thought. Even wounded, she could do better than that.
"What's your name, neighbor?"

"I'm Joel," he said. "Joel Summer."

In the soft lamplight spilling onto the porch, Maggie could make out a hard-planed face and very dark,
straight hair. The shadow view was promising enough
that she wished for better light. "What do you do,
Joel?"

He shifted again, crossing powerful arms over a
deep chest. "I work at the raptor center."

"Raptors are birds, right?" she asked with a frown.

"Big birds." He grinned. "Eagles and falcons and
hawks. Owls."

She cocked her head. "That's an unusual career."
The natural curiosity that had led her into newspapers prompted her next question. "How did you get
into that?"

"I don't remember a time when I didn't love birds.
As soon as I learned you could earn a living studying
them, I knew what I was going to do."

Maggie smiled. "You're one of the lucky ones, then."

"'Lucky'?" There was a distinct edge of bitter humor in the echo.

"'Blessed is he who has found his work,'" she quoted. "'Let him ask no other blessedness.'" Maggie lifted her beer in a toast. "Carlyle," she added.

"Nice theory," he said.

Maggie heard the faintest tinge of resignation in his voice. "It's not everything you'd hoped?"

"My work never disappoints me." Again his grin flashed at Maggie, and she wondered if she'd imagined the other resignation. "Did you know a prairie falcon can fly 150 miles an hour?"

"No." She smiled.

He smiled, too. "They're the most graceful creatures God ever created."

"Are falcons your favorites, then?"

"No, I don't think I have a favorite." He made a gesture with one hand. "They're all—" he shook his head slightly "—magnificent. There's no other word for them."

The phone rang inside Maggie's apartment, and she stood up quickly. The motion sent a quick, sharp wave of dizziness through her brain and she stopped, blinking until her vision cleared, one hand over her wounded eye.

Joel crossed to her in an instant, bracing her with a strong grip on her arm. "Are you all right?"

She nodded as the dizziness passed, lifting the beer ruefully. "Maybe I should have stuck to apple juice tonight." She glanced up at him, about to offer her thanks, but for one split second, less time than passed between the summoning rings of the telephone, Maggie was utterly awestruck.

For the man looking down at her with concern was more than huge, although he was that—he towered over her five foot ten. He was also fiercely beautiful in the yellow light coming through her screen door. Up close, the hard planes of his face were aligned in perfect symmetry, blunt cheek bones angling to a nose that was large but somehow right in his strong face. A hard-cut jaw led to a square chin below firm, sculpted lips, and his broad brow was broken with careless scatters of dark hair.

All of that would have been enough to make any sane woman take a second glance, but his eyes caught and pinned her where she stood. They were a vivid, electric blue and as clear as the spring night, eyes almost too large for a man's face, eyes that would see everything, always.

Maggie started as the phone rang again. "I'd better get that before it wakes my daughter," she said, her voice surprisingly even. "It was nice to meet you."

He nodded, releasing her arm. "You, too."

Maggie hurried inside, catching the phone on the fourth ring. It was Sharon, needing advice about the editorial page, which was ordinarily Maggie's responsibility. Maggie gave her the stats she needed and asked, "How's it going?"

"If you don't think this is one of the best issues we've ever done, I'll eat my hat."

"Thanks, Sharon." She threaded her fingers through her hair. "You know I trust you."

"You're just a worrywart. That's the trouble with you self-sufficient types—you can't delegate."

Maggie grinned. "I delegated, okay? I promise I won't call later."

"Get some rest. I'll see you Friday."

As she hung up, once more firmly anchored in reality, she glanced over her shoulder toward the front door and smiled. It had been a long time since a man had made her mouth drop. She shook her head and turned off lights on the ground floor. Not even a man that gorgeous could jolt her out of her exhaustion tonight.

But as she climbed the stairs toward her bedroom, she wondered what it might have been like to offer him a beer and chat a little longer in the comfort of darkness.

Joel lingered on the porch after she had gone inside, reveling in the soft night and first insect noises of the year. Her company would have been welcome, but the night, too, was good—clear and full of stars. The gentle air fed his skin. His life had been void of such simple pleasures for a long, long time. He didn't take them for granted.

The lights in the apartment next to his clicked out, leaving him in a deeper night. The tape that had been playing on his stereo had reached its end. Around the side of the house, he heard a cat meow raggedly several times, and overhead, a rustling in an elm signaled a squirrel or a bird.

Maggie, he thought. The name suited her in ways he hadn't dreamed it would, suited her sturdy movements and the strength in her arms and legs.

The ragged meow of the cat sounded again, and frowning, Joel got up to investigate. It sounded hurt or hungry or weak. He peered into the bushes along the house and called softly in the accepted fashion, wondering, not for the first time, if the sounds used to coax an animal were universal or just American. "Here, kitty, kitty, kitty."

Deep in the bushes, Joel saw a flash of round eyes, and the cat wandered out, a big black-and-white tom with matted fur and a notched ear. He croaked another meow, looking at Joel with wary hope.

Joel made no sudden move. Instead, he spoke to the stray in a soft, even voice. "Somebody left you behind, didn't they? I always hate that." Slowly, he crouched and reached a hand through the rails. "I won't hurt you."

The cat shied, and giving Joel one more glance, dashed back into the bushes.

"You'll be back," Joel said, his heart tight. "You'll see."

Thursdays were Maggie's only certain day off, and she reveled in the chance to sleep late and start the day as lazily as she could. A little after one, her grandmother came over with a copy of the *Wanderer* and a rich selection of pastries in a square white bakery box to share over coffee. It was a Thursday afternoon ritual.

Since she hadn't seen the paper yet, Maggie was particularly glad to see her grandmother. "I was so worried this wouldn't get out on time," she said, eagerly snatching the tabloid-size weekly.

"Goodness, child," Anna said in her Texas-shaded drawl. "What in the world happened to you?"

"Oh, I forgot you hadn't seen me. Come on." Maggie led the way through the living room to her spacious, sunny kitchen before she answered, shaking open the paper as she walked. When she saw the photo covering a solid three-quarters of the front page, she grinned, turning to show her grandmother. "This is what happened," she said with a chortle. "Isn't that gorgeous?"

Anna, dressed in a pale green shirtwaist dress with splashes of pinkish flowers, made a clucking noise. She poured a cup of coffee. "I suppose you were right in the thick of it."

"Not intentionally, but yes, that's where I ended up." Maggie smiled as she examined the photo more closely, a good action shot of the crowd, with the demonstrators in the background and an angry boy in leather raising a fist in the foreground. His fist pointed perfectly to the hand-lettered sign in the background that read End Violence in Our Music. Ban Proud Fox. "Beautiful," Maggie said with a sigh. "The kids are going to love it."

"Which kids?"

"My readers, Grandma. The ones that buy the paper, remember?"

"Well," sniffed Anna, "I think it looks like you support that vile music. You're giving this whole thing so much attention."

"You know better." It was old ground. The war over the band Proud Fox had been raging for two months. "I think they write reprehensible lyrics and that they're not behaving responsibly. But you know what they say about free speech. It's not free unless everybody has it."

Anna opened the box of pastries. "No sense in us arguing about it again." A frown wrinkled her pale white skin as she arranged the sweet rolls on a plate, then took a seat at the table. "That cut looks pretty serious, Maggie. Are you sure you're all right?"

"Fine." Maggie paused to look at herself in the mirror behind her plant shelf. Aside from the neat arch that sliced through her eyebrow, extending an inch into her forehead, she also had a colorful black eye. She brushed her straight, tawny hair away from the wound and turned back to her grandmother. "I'll live." She selected a cheese Danish from the plate on the table and sat down. "Better me than Samantha."

"She was there?"

"Wearing a leather jacket, yet."

"Ye gods. See what I mean?"

Maggie chose her words carefully. "None of this would be happening if those who didn't like the band ignored it." The Danish was perfect, and Maggie sighed. "Sam's just going through some kind of identity crisis or something right now."

"Are you going to let her stay with her dad this summer?"

"Of course I am."

Anna dabbed her mouth with a paper napkin, her cornflower-blue eyes snapping as she gazed at her granddaughter. "He's no good for her."

"I disagree." Maggie straightened in her chair and cocked her head, puzzled. "Are you angry with me about something? You're not exactly cheerful today."

For a moment, Anna measured Maggie. "I'm worried about you. I don't like this job, and I think you've got more than you can handle in your stepdaughter, and you won't accept help from anybody." She stood up briskly and carried her coffee cup to the counter. She paused there for a moment. "I spoke with your mother this morning."

Aha, Maggie thought.

"She's talking about divorce again."

Maggie eyed a bear claw, trying to decide whether to have a second. "Big surprise."

"I didn't raise her to be like this. Three marriages, all in the dumps. What's wrong with her?"

"Well, I can't speak for the second and third, but my father was *not* a gem of a man," Maggie said. "I think she was brave to stick it out for the twenty years she did." What Maggie's mother did was her own business. The two had never been close, and over time had drifted apart to the point that they corresponded only infrequently. If pressed, she would have said she loved her mother but that they had nothing at all in common. Maggie's true parent was—and always had been—her grandmother.

She went to Anna and hugged her. "Mom's a big girl now, and you did the best you could. Let the rest go."

Anna nodded, and when Maggie released her, peered out the window over the sink. "How are the lilacs doing this year?"

Maggie poured a second cup of coffee and glanced out. "Not quite open yet, but they'll be pretty in a few days."

"Who's that man out there, Maggie?" Anna said sharply.

Maggie felt her heart flip oddly as she leaned over, bumping Anna's shoulder as they both looked out the window. There, admiring the buds on a semicircular bank of lilac bushes, was her new neighbor. "Joel Summer," she said quietly. He wore shorts this afternoon, and his legs, Maggie thought, were a sight to behold—winter pale but sturdy and corded with muscle. His hair in the daylight was dark chestnut, flicking sparks of deep red light when he moved his head.

As she watched, a stray tomcat wandered through the yard, a cat as big, in his own way, as the man who crouched to call him.

"Good luck," Maggie said. The cat had been mistreated at some point, then left behind to fend for itself. It wandered the streets, slept on convenient porch swings, accepted food when it was offered but disdained human touch.

"What a scruffy cat," commented Anna.

"I feel sorry for him," Maggie said, and smiled, for in spite of Joel's cajoling, the black-and-white cat veered off to the left and plopped down in a patch of grassy sunlight. Joel stared at him for a moment, then stood and went back into his house.

A minute later, he emerged with a can of tuna. He carried it toward the cat, talking and approaching slowly. A few feet away, he put the can down and backed off to squat nearby.

The cat was antisocial but far from stupid. As if expecting a blow at any minute, he moved toward the can, keeping an eye on Joel, who continued to talk to the animal but didn't move. It ate with the kind of desperation born of long-term hunger, gobbling as quickly as he could.

"That's kinda sweet," Anna said.

Maggie nodded. "He seems like a nice person— works with eagles and hawks, he said."

Anna lifted an eyebrow teasingly. "More than just nice," she teased. Her laugh was surprisingly ribald and bold, coming from the mouth of such a refined-looking woman.

"Come on away from the window, Gram," Maggie said dryly. "We have to watch your blood pressure."

"Oh," Anna said, disappointment thick in her words. "The cat ran off, got scared."

Maggie glanced back out. Joel hadn't moved and he watched the departing cat with a pensive expression on his face. She looked at her grandmother. "I have to admit he's good-looking."

"Now *you* come on away from the window," Anna said. "Don't want your blood pressure going up."

"Oh, please," Maggie protested, and laughed as she took her chair. "Men are like flowers, strictly for admiring."

Anna halted in the center of the kitchen, hands on her hips. Maggie thought her grandmother was about to offer some proverbial injunction about the comforts of a husband in old age. Instead, she let go of another ripe laugh. "If you think looking at a man like that is enough, you've been working too hard."

Maggie rolled her eyes and picked up the bear claw. "Forget it, Gram. I'm not interested. Men are terrific for about six months, then you have start picking up socks and changing the channel so they can watch their ball games." She wrinkled her nose. "And they all want you to cook. Ugh." With a grin, she added, "Sharon calls it PMS—Permanent Male Syndrome."

Anna nodded appreciatively, her cornflower eyes sparkling. Then she patted her white collar into place. "The right man can make it all worthwhile."

"Hmm..." Maggie murmured. As she focused on the flavor of brown sugar and pecans, she remembered the way Joel had described a prairie falcon in his resonant voice, the way he had searched for a word to describe the birds he worked with.

She heard his voice utter the word again. *Magnificent.*

Resolutely, she shut it out. "What else did my mother have to say this morning?"

Chapter Two

Late Friday night, Joel heard the waffling rumble of souped-up cars on the street outside. A car door slammed, and shortly afterward the front door next to his own was opened and closed.

Moments later, a high, hysterical teenage voice raised in protestation seeped through his walls. Although he turned up the late movie, a rare showing of *The Maltese Falcon*, he could still make out an argument. Only the tone drifted through, but even that made Joel feel like a spy. After a few moments, he clicked off the television and headed out the back door.

Outside, cool air touched his bare forearms. He stretched hard and settled on the steps, leaning backward on his elbows to look at the sky. Just over the treetops loomed the shadow of the mountains, their tips twinkling with the red lights of radio and television towers. Higher, stars shone brilliantly in a sky free of dingy pollutants, thanks to a rain that afternoon.

It was a pattern he had forgotten in his years away—the clouds that rolled in with an ominous rumbling by four every day throughout the spring and early summer. Some days, lightning cracked and burst as the rain fell in torrents for twenty or thirty minutes. Other days, there would be a whispering of moisture, like a mist. Always, the clouds moved on by dinnertime, leaving the air fresh, the night sky sparkling. He let his head fall back in thankfulness, thinking perhaps he would find a telescope somewhere.

The back door twin to his own suddenly slammed. Joel straightened curiously. A figure moved into sight. Maggie. Her heavy, honey-colored hair shone around her shoulders, and she wore a straight cotton skirt with a simple, long-sleeved T-shirt. She collapsed on the back steps, dropping her head to her knees in a posture of defeat.

Now what? Joel thought. She obviously hadn't seen him. He didn't want to startle or embarrass her.

He coughed.

Her head flew up and she turned toward him. "You scared me," she said. She stood up.

Joel jumped to his feet. "You don't have to go." He'd been restless and hungry for company all evening. "It's your backyard, too."

She smiled, acknowledging the reference to her words earlier in the week.

He crossed the grassy area between them and stood at the foot of her stairs. "I can offer you a beer," he said with a quick lift of his eyebrows.

For an instant, Maggie said nothing. He was close enough that she could have stretched out a hand to touch his powerful shoulders beneath the blue cotton. There was something oddly familiar about him, something she couldn't quite place. "Do I know you from somewhere?" she asked.

"Another life." His words held only the barest note of teasing, so that for a moment she couldn't tell if he was serious or not. The amusement on his face gave him away.

Maggie laughed. "Oh, yes. You were that wretched sea captain."

"Were you my promised bride?"

"No." She lifted her chin. "Your maiden aunt, irritated with you for running off to sea and leaving your mother a nervous wreck."

He grinned and his rather severe features were transformed into an irresistibly boyish expression. Dimples, she noted with an inward sigh. How could one man have been gifted with such an array of physical perfections?

"Let me make it up to you, Auntie," he said.

"And well you should," she returned.

"I'll be back in a flash." He gave a salute and a bow.

As soon as he departed, Maggie wondered what she was doing. But the choice was a simple one—stay outside in the company of another adult or go inside and listen to Samantha weep over her punishment. She sank back down onto the steps.

Joel returned with two long-necked bottles of beer. "I never could resist a woman who drank her beer from the bottle," he said with a smile, handing her one.

"That sounds like an innuendo," Maggie said.

He laughed. "No, that's not what I meant."

"In that case," she said with a smile, "thanks for the reassurance. I keep trying to develop a ladylike taste for Chablis or cognac, but I can't seem to pull it off." She sipped gingerly. "Old habits die hard. I started drinking beer in college and never have found anything I liked as well."

"Beer's got heart."

"I guess it does." He stood at the bottom of the steps and Maggie shifted, gesturing toward the lower stair. "You can sit down if you like."

"Thanks." He settled just below her and immediately seemed to fill every available inch of space. The shapely arms and broad thighs crowded her field of vision, and as he relaxed on one elbow, his forearm warmed her shin without quite touching it.

"So," she said, trying to distract herself, "how are you doing with the cat?"

"You mean the old tom?"

"I saw you with the can of tuna yesterday."

Joel sighed. "He's a tough case." He looked at Maggie. "Do you know anything about him?"

"He's been around as long as I've lived here—about two years. I feed him in the wintertime." She pointed to a loose board on the cellar door. "And he crawls in there when it's cold."

"He's probably been abused."

"Poor thing. I wish you luck." She frowned. "I thought you were a bird man. Why would you want to save a cat?"

A throaty chuckle rumbled into the still night. "The kind of birds I'm interested in would make short work of that cat."

Maggie smiled. "I guess I'm used to Tweety and Sylvester."

"That cat probably can't kill birds anymore, anyway. Even if he could, I wouldn't dislike cats just because they hunt birds." He looked up to the treetops, as if seeing doomed prey. "A robin kills a worm, a cat kills a robin, an eagle carries off a cat—it's the natural cycle."

"That's a terrible thought," Maggie protested.

He looked up at her, his clear eyes sober. "Not really," he said. "When you can see the overall design of nature, the checks and balances, the predators and the prey, it's incredible." He paused, giving a sad twist to his lips. "It's only when mighty humanity gets involved that the balance falls completely out of whack."

"You know," Maggie said. "It's funny you're bringing that up—I thought so much about pollution this past winter." She leaned forward. "On the days the carbon monoxide looked like fog on the ground, I kept worrying about the prairie dogs and the squirrels and all those other little creatures that had no idea why they couldn't breathe. I kept wondering what would happen to them." She laughed. "Naturally, I interviewed an expert for a story."

"I'm sorry I missed reading it." He inclined his head. "As terrible as things seem right now, people are a lot more aware of ecology than they were thirty years ago. I like to think that's progress."

"Too bad it took such dramatic illustrations to get our attention."

"No, we just have to go from here." He straightened abruptly and his arm grazed her leg as he lifted his beer, then he glanced almost shyly at Maggie over his shoulder. "Don't get me going on this," he warned. "I'll climb right up on my soapbox and start making speeches. You're a good listener."

"Not always," she said honestly.

"I'll wager, just the same, that you write the advice column in your newspaper."

Maggie laughed. "Guilty."

"Those kids ask some tough questions—questions I don't know if I could answer."

"It's easy when you're not involved," she said, thinking of Samantha with a pang. Maggie had overreacted tonight. She'd even realized it in the middle of the argument, but by that time Samantha had been half-hysterical and there had been no choice but to send her to her room to cry it off.

Samantha was hiding something. And it hurt. No matter how well Maggie had succeeded in walling herself off from the rest of the world, she couldn't help feeling a sharp stab of sorrow over her daughter's dishonesty. It hurt to know that Samantha thought she couldn't trust her.

Joel said nothing as Maggie drifted, obviously awash in deep thoughts he had no wish to disturb. Instead, he enjoyed the opportunity to study her. Her skin was tawny, even so early in the year, and in spite of the bruises and stitches surrounding her left eye, he thought she was exotic and wild looking, with almond eyes and unusual slants in her face. Not everyone would think she was beautiful, he felt sure—but he wasn't everyone.

Her mouth turned down as she mulled her problem, and with a weary gesture, she reached back to gather her hair into a ponytail, which she held loosely in her hand. The movement showed her graceful neck and the lobe of an ear pierced with an earring that shone golden against her flesh. Joel felt a restlessness stir in his belly, an almost forgotten sensation of desire.

She looked at him suddenly as if reading his vaguely carnal perusal. "Sorry," she said, "I went off on a little walk of my own."

"That's all right." He smiled.

"How long have you worked with your birds?" Maggie asked, more comfortable shifting the conversation away from herself.

"A long time—off and on." He glanced at his hands.

Maggie sensed again his disillusionment or sorrow, but his tone of voice made it clear this line of conversation was a dead end. She studied him wordlessly. No matter what she'd told her grandmother about men, there was a lot more to Joel than the ability to grace the scenery. In fact, when she listened to him talk, she felt ashamed for assigning him such a trivial function.

Still, it was hard to ignore his physical presence. From where she sat, the long column of his tanned throat showed at the open neck of his shirt, and she could see the whorl at his crown that governed the way his thick hair grew. Her gaze fell on his lips, full and firm and ripe. She allowed her gaze to linger for the barest instant, then looked away.

"Listen," he said, touching her shin with his fingers. "I think I hear the cat."

Maggie lifted her head. From the cove of lilac bushes toward the back of the yard came the unmistakable sound of the tom's call, a meow so worn it sounded like a piano with half the keys missing.

"That's my cue," Joel said, standing. He paused, looking at her. "I enjoy your company, Maggie. I hope we'll have another chance to talk again soon."

"So do I." She stood almost reluctantly and smiled. "Good night."

She carried her bottle inside and threw it away, then combed through the cabinets, trying to find her stash of sour-cream-and-onion potato chips. For a minute, she thought Sam might have found them, and then she remembered where they were—in the closet with the built-in ironing board. She took a soda and the chips with her as she checked the doors and closed any curtains that had been missed.

Joel, she thought as she automatically performed the duties. What woman couldn't spin a fantasy about a man like that? Intelligent and warm and strong and handsome—the perfect man for cologne advertising.

As she headed upstairs, she wondered cynically what the catch was. That age-old fantasy of a strong and gentle man was terrific, but in her experience, real men didn't come in that combination.

After her divorce, Maggie had resolved to play it smart with men, and for practical purposes she had divided them into three categories: macho, weak or charming. Her father had been a macho man, insistent upon his own way, and when he hadn't gotten it, he'd resorted to whatever means necessary to get it.

The second category, the weak men, were a little more rare. To this group Maggie relegated all the men who were intimidated by her height or her directness, men who found themselves at a loss for words when Maggie threw down the gauntlet of a debate. Nothing, in her opinion, was more aggravating than a man who couldn't stand on his own two feet in the face of an opponent.

Between the two categories fell the charming ones—articulate, often handsome men who'd learned how to give a woman the appearance of what she needed without actually giving anything of themselves. Paul had fallen into that category. He was accomplished and good-looking, even warm when he chose to be.

The problem with her ex-husband had been his need to exercise his charm over any woman he felt to be worthy of the challenge.

But she'd long since forgiven Paul. At twenty, she'd been unable to see what now was plain: Paul had never overcome his grief over losing his beloved first wife— Samantha's mother. Instead, he ran into the arms of women who chased away her ghost.

Joel, now, didn't seem to fit into any of the categories previously developed. Macho men didn't try to tame stray cats. Weak men wouldn't state their opinions as clearly as he had about ecology. Charming men—well, he might fall into that category. She bit her lip in consideration. No, she decided. He seemed too sincere.

So, since she prided herself on open-mindedness, she created a new category. He'd be the first member of her new file of sincere men. Since he was the first one, she didn't know what the accompanying flaws were, but one thing was certain: there *would* be flaws.

She stopped at Samantha's door. Seeing the light spilling across the carpet through the crack, she knocked softly. "Can I come in?"

A muffled "Yes" came through, and Maggie opened the door.

Sam, dressed in an ancient T-shirt and gray sweats, her hair tumbled around her face, lay across the bed. Her eyes were swollen and red with crying. "Are you all right?" Maggie asked.

Samantha nodded miserably.

Maggie sat gingerly on the edge of the bed. "Look, I overreacted in anger. I'm sorry I yelled at you."

"I know." Her voice was small.

"The truth is, Sam, my feelings are hurt because you've just decided I'm not going to understand or approve of whatever it is that you're hiding, without giving me a chance."

Sam picked at the blue flowers on her bedspread and said nothing.

Maggie sighed. "I'm going to have to trust you to tell me when you think the time is right, I guess. In the meantime, you will be on time when I give you curfew, and I will not tolerate lies about who you're with. Your restriction stands."

"Yes, ma'am."

At the door, Maggie paused, waffling over her next words. She didn't want to seem as if she were rewarding Samantha's bad behavior; at the same time, she'd been planning a surprise of epic proportions for more than a month, and it had been scheduled for tomorrow afternoon.

Treat the behavior, not the person, she decided. "I've been planning something for you, and it's set to happen tomorrow. I'd like to take you to lunch."

"I thought you were mad at me."

"I was. I'm not now," Maggie said. "But more than angry, I was worried. You've been punished and I hope you won't disregard my rules again." She took a breath. "That doesn't mean I don't like you and I don't want to be with you."

Samantha sat up, tears trickling down her face. "I don't know why you keep putting up with me."

Maggie laughed softly. "Because I love you, silly girl. That's a mother's job."

"I'm not much of a daughter sometimes."

"Unfortunately, that's sometimes a daughter's job."

Samantha smiled wanly.

"It's time to get some sleep. I'll see you in the morning," said Maggie gently.

Sam stopped her. "I'm sorry, Maggie. I'll tell you tomorrow, okay?"

"Fair enough. Good night."

"'Night."

In her own bedroom, Maggie turned on a small lamp. This was her sanctuary, the reason she had rented the apartment two years before, and the source of her sanity. The proportions were huge. Three long windows opened onto the garden on one side of the room, and two more showed the gently waving branches of a cottonwood tree. On the opposite wall was a huge closet, and a small glassed-in room holding a desk and her work space jutted out from beyond the bed. In the summertime, she opened all the windows to smell the fragrance of the roses that climbed over the outside of the house.

Over the hardwood floor were scattered imitation Persian and Oriental rugs in shades of pale blue with red. A cherry bed with heavy posts dominated the middle of the room. At the windows hung curtains of delicate bone-colored lace. One overstuffed chair sat by the long windows overlooking the backyard, and a single photograph of Samantha at the age of seven—taken by Maggie on an outing to the zoo—sat on the small cherry table next to the chair.

On a low table opposite her chair, looking completely out of place, was a primitive VCR and a cabinet of tapes stacked on top of an old floor-model television. She'd claimed both for her personal use when Paul had given them a newer model last Christmas.

She kept potpourris of woods herbs in brass containers around the room, and tonight the subtle scent relaxed her, as it always did. Going to the VCR, she selected a tape at random, turned the TV on to warm up and turned off her lamp. Then she sank into the overstuffed easy chair in front of the windows, opened her soda and used the remote to start the tape.

"What's it going to be tonight, Captain Kirk?" The opening credits to *Star Trek* flashed—"A Requiem for Methuselah." One of her favorites.

The tapes were all *Star Trek*, a show she'd been too young to enjoy when it had originally run on network television. During the past two years, she'd managed to tape almost every episode—thankfully just as the syndicate stations that had been running it took it off their schedules.

About halfway through the program, Maggie realized a shadow on the grass outside had been nagging her peripheral vision for quite some time. At the commercial, she left the tape running at normal speed and looked out to investigate.

The yard was dark except for a long rectangle of light that Maggie assumed fell from the windowed alcove of Joel's bedroom. It was there that Maggie had seen the shadow from the corner of her eye.

There on the grass fell the silhouette of a man in few, if any, clothes. She would have known it was Joel anywhere, with those shoulders and the fine sculpted thighs. The rest, as he stretched his arms above his head, froze her in position, and although she hated herself for staring, for invading his privacy like that, she couldn't look away.

One shadow arm reached out to the wall, and the square of light abruptly disappeared. Maggie caught herself leaning forward. "Oh, grow up, Maggie," she said aloud, falling back into her chair.

As she tried to engross herself once again in the adventures of the U.S.S. *Enterprise*, her throat was dry. Face it, woman, she told herself. Sour-cream-and-onion potato chips can only take you so far. The same thing applied to work and *Star Trek*. They simply couldn't fill the gap she sometimes felt, because what she missed was the pleasure a woman could find only with a man.

For one excruciating minute, she allowed herself the rare luxury of imagining the two things she most often missed—the taste of a man's lips and the heady scent of him as he held her.

It wasn't memories of Paul she found in her mind, however. Instead, she imagined what the tastes and smells of Joel Summer might be.

At the end of the moment that she allowed herself, she firmly returned her attention to the television screen and potato chips. But when she realized fifteen minutes later that she'd consumed the entire bag of chips, she knew it was only her conscious mind she'd convinced to occupy itself with something besides the shivery attraction she felt toward the new neighbor. Her subconscious definitely had other plans.

The next morning, in anticipation of her lunch with Samantha and the surprise she had been hoarding for her daughter, Maggie donned a rust-colored skirt and blouse that suited the angularity of her face and body. It was her very favorite ensemble, and as the nubby cloth settled comfortably around her, she wished everything she owned made her feel as good as it did. Even her black eye seemed to look a little better, in spite of the spidery stitches dissecting her eyebrow. When she dabbed makeup over the bruises, she thought she looked almost normal.

The scent of fresh onions and coffee led her to the kitchen, where she found Samantha, already up and dressed, cooking breakfast. "Morning," Sam said cheerfully.

"Good morning," Maggie replied. "You look almost as good as that food smells." Although Maggie hated the overly teased and curled hairstyle Samantha insisted upon, the rest was true. Her daughter had remarkably creamy skin and deep emerald eyes. Around her neck was tied a silky maroon scarf. Maggie tugged it teasingly. "I love what you do with scarves."

"Thanks." Sam stirred the potatoes. "You don't seem very surprised that I cooked your breakfast."

Maggie poured a cup of coffee and grinned. "I'm not. You always cook when you want to make amends."

"Do I?"

"And whenever you want a special favor."

Sam flashed a coy smile.

"Not that I mind, you understand," Maggie continued, stealing a mouthful of hash browns from the pan with a fork. "I will never, as long as I live, learn to like cooking."

"And it shows. I feel sorry for your stomach when I go to Dad's."

Maggie laughed, unable to be offended at so obvious a fact. "I manage."

Sam rolled her eyes. "I would think even you would get sick of cheeseburgers eventually."

"Afraid not—better a cheeseburger made by someone else than a gourmet meal made by me." She got out the table settings. "And, anyway, I'm supposed to be nagging *you* about food, not the other way around."

"Most people's mothers don't eat like you do," Sam said, carrying the pan to the table to serve the lightly browned potatoes.

"And not everyone wants to be a model." The eggs, too, were perfect. Maggie didn't wait for Samantha to return to the table. She sat down at the steaming plate to satisfy her rumbling stomach.

Sam had taken typically skimpy portions, and Maggie knew they'd be unsalted. Whatever else happened, Samantha was very focused upon the perfect health she knew she needed to achieve a modeling career. It was the single largest reason Maggie never worried about drugs—Samantha was obsessive about the idea of modeling.

And she thought Sam had every reason to aspire to such a career. A shaft of gentle morning sunlight fingered one flawless cheek and edged the straight slope of her nose; it threw in shadow a ripe, red mouth and tipped thick lashes. She was also a tall girl, with the beginnings of a shapely figure and an easy grace of movement. Whether she could make it in the cutthroat world of modeling remained to be seen, but there was certainly a good amount of raw material.

Samantha caught Maggie staring. "What?"

Maggie dipped her head to take a sip of coffee. "Nothing." She dabbed her lips with a napkin. "You're going to love your surprise."

Sam jutted out her chin stubbornly. "I'm not going to bite this time. You always tease me forever before you spring it, so I'm going to just wait and see."

"Just for that," Maggie said with a grin, "I'm going to stretch it out double."

"Go ahead," she said airily.

"I will." Maggie devoured her eggs, liberally seasoned with Tabasco and salt and pepper. "Sam, you're a wonderful cook."

"Thanks." The word was perfunctory, and Maggie glanced at her daughter.

"Okay, are you ready?" Sam said, putting her fork down on her plate.

Maggie swallowed. She sat up, feeling cold worry race up her spine. What if this revelation was something awful? "Shoot," she said.

Sam licked her lips and raised her eyes. "I'm in love."

"And?"

"I don't think you are going to like him. At all."

Maggie nodded. "Why not?"

"He's the boy I went to the demonstration with. It was his jacket I was wearing when I first saw you in the crowd."

A speed rocker, Maggie thought, stomach sinking. Her imagination conjured up a quick example of the very worst of the breed, a surly, wild-haired youth, with a cigarette in one hand and a bottle of booze in the other. She fingered the handle of her coffee cup, buying time to hide her instinctual reaction. "Tell me about him."

"Well..." Sam glanced up toward the ceiling, a silly smile creeping across her face, a smile she tried to hold in. Maggie quelled an urge to shake her head—Sam was not given to silliness over boys.

"His name is David," she said, her eyes going soft. "He's sixteen and he's in my English class."

Maggie nodded, finally daring to take another bite of her eggs. "Does he drive?"

"He has his license, but he doesn't have a car. He's working," she hastened to add. "At a restaurant."

"When can I meet him?"

Sam glanced at her plate. "As soon as my restriction is over. I promise."

"Great." She reached over the table to touch Samantha's hand. "I'll do my best to be fair."

"I know."

The daughter was going to be a beauty, Joel thought. No doubt about it. She was a little sullen, as girls often are at that age. Suspicious, too, as she caught sight of him working on his ten-speed on the porch. Her mother had run back inside to fetch some forgotten something, and the girl waited at the edge of the porch with her arms crossed, staring at him. Joel looked back at her. "Hi," he said.

"You must be the new neighbor," she replied, her voice thick with the disdain of one well acquainted with new neighbors and other such insects.

He grinned and turned back to his task. "Guess so," he agreed, scraping the bike wheel with slow strokes.

The girl made a small dismissive sound and turned away. At that moment, Maggie slammed the front door shut.

Joel looked up... and caught his breath. He'd only seen her with night disguising her features, and even then, she'd been attractive. In the full light of day, dressed well and carefully made-up, she reminded him of a tiger. Her heavy hair swung around her shoulders in honey fluidness, and her tawny skin was high-lighted by the rich rust of her clothing. Her body was long, full at the hip, less so at the breast, a shape women despised, a fact Joel had never understood. Without consciously knowing that he did so, he stood up. "Hi, Maggie," he said.

Maggie turned at the depth and heat of his throaty words, reacting to the sound in spite of her quick rush to halt the response. When she met his eyes, it was impossible to mistake the expression she saw there—a leaping male appreciation. In a tone that sounded considerably more calm than she felt, she said, "Hi, Joel." She shifted her sweater in her arms. "Are you a bike enthusiast?"

His eyes, a riotous blue in the sunlight, burned into her, and Maggie couldn't help remembering his shadow on the grass last night. Her gaze strayed for the briefest second to his well-cut lips before darting back to the steady look fastened upon her. He had noticed, and his eyes swept down to her lips in return. Maggie would have sworn she could feel the exact instant they lit upon her lower lip.

But the moment was fleeting. When he said, "Yes, I am," in reply to her question, she wasn't sure what that question had been. At a loss, she nodded.

"Are you coming, Mother?" Sam prodded, halfway down the sidewalk to the car.

Maggie flashed a grin at Joel. "I've been summoned."

"So I see," he said, returning her smile. "Have a good time."

"You, too." Kicking herself for the banality of her reply, she hurried down the walk.

Joel watched the car until it disappeared around the corner. He still held the bike wheel in his hand, forgotten. How long had it been since a woman had shaken him like the glorious Maggie?

Longer than he could remember. He grinned to himself, finding he liked the sensation of blood speeding into forgotten portions of his anatomy, enjoyed the way his nerves tingled with new awareness.

Generally, he was wary with women, unwilling to risk the betrayals they could perpetuate. But Maggie—

Her mind had been exactly what he'd expected: solid and keen and sympathetic. All he'd hoped for in her physical appearance was a woman he could look upon easily.

Kneeling to affix the wheel to his bike, he shook his head. It was almost incredible how much more she was. This morning the sight of her had made his palms sweaty, his knees weak. It made his gamble all the more exciting.

And the daughter made it more dangerous. A hint of guilt touched him as he considered the dilemma her unexpected presence caused him. He mulled it only briefly.

The game had already begun, and his hand was dealt. With a wry grin, he realized the high stakes had him whistling. Penny-ante had been his game all his life. He'd never realized the thrill to be had in the big time.

Chapter Three

As Maggie climbed into the car, Sam said, "Looks like I'm not the only one who's got a new boyfriend."

"I only met him a few days ago," Maggie said, starting the car.

"He's pretty taken with you."

"Hardly, Samantha," she said coolly.

"Oh, please," Samantha said with an air of superiority. "You guys did everything but shuffle your feet."

A hot flush of embarrassment touched Maggie's cheeks. Had it really been that obvious? Maybe she'd been working with teenagers too long, she thought darkly. Now she was beginning to act like one. Next she'd be sending him a note in hot purple ink, the *i*'s dotted with tiny hearts.

She ignored the subject after that, as she and Samantha spent the morning wandering around the booths set up in Acacia Park in the heart of Colorado Springs, exploring the displays of arts and crafts, the paintings and performance artists.

Late in the morning, Samantha fell under the spell of a bagpipe that a man in a kilt and a red beard played with considerable skill. Maggie wandered into a booth nearby to admire the handwoven goods, and engaged in a long conversation with the weaver about the merits of various materials and styles. When the woman praised Maggie's cotton skirt and blouse, then hunted out a heavy shawl in tones of russet and gold to complement it, Maggie couldn't resist the purchase and went off smiling broadly.

Joining Sam, still entranced, she nudged her. "Are you ready to get some lunch?"

Sam cocked her head. "What about my surprise?"

"After lunch. We're going to meet Sharon then."

"Okay." She shrugged, feigning indifference, and they headed off. "Can we eat at Michelle's?"

"As if you'd pick any other place."

Sam flashed a grin that transformed her sullen prettiness into a gleam of impishness. "I just give you an excuse to indulge your sweet tooth."

"You look five years old when you grin like that."

"Ornery, right?"

"Heavens yes. You ran me a merry chase the first year."

"I did?" Sam stopped at the corner. "What changed it?"

Maggie focused on the pedestrian light. "You got chicken pox," she said. "And I mean you *really* got chicken pox. Couldn't move for days, fever through the roof. Your dad was on assignment in Israel, and I had to handle you myself." They stepped off the curb. "When you got well, you were still ornery, but I guess you'd decided I'd be an okay mom."

Sam absorbed this without speaking, but as she gained the opposite curb, she burst out, "I remember that!" She turned to Maggie, grabbing her arm. "You let me suck on those root beer candy sticks all day, and when I got well, you took me to the carnival to celebrate."

Maggie nodded. "That's the time."

"How cool." Then she pressed a hand to her cheek. "Thank goodness I didn't get scars. There's a girl in my school with a chicken pox scar right in the middle of her forehead."

"Oh, it's rare. You have some, though, I'm sure."

"Where?"

They reached the restaurant. With her hand on the glass door, Maggie whispered, "Your bottom."

Samantha giggled.

In spite of the crowds at the park, they were able to get a table fairly quickly. Michelle's was known mainly for its chocolates and ice cream delights, but they served an interesting variety of other foods, as well. Maggie ordered a Monte Cristo sandwich; Samantha a Greek salad with feta cheese. Throughout the meal, a series of Greek folk music selections poured over the speaker system.

"When my grandmother used to bring me here," Maggie commented, "I thought it was the most magical place in the world." She smiled. "We used to come on Sunday afternoons when I visited over Christmas vacations. She let me order anything I wanted from the pastry cart, but I had to be able to name it."

"That sounds like Grandma. She wouldn't buy me a pair of dress shoes until I found a purse that would match them." She popped a long olive into her mouth. "She's really into all that ladylike stuff."

"But she's nearly seventy, and I can't think of anyone with more natural elegance. You could do worse than to follow in her footsteps."

"You're pretty elegant, too, Maggie," Sam said. "When you're not in one of your back-to-nature moods."

Maggie shrugged. "Different styles for different days." She motioned to the waitress. "I'll let you pick a pastry if you can name it," she said to Samantha.

"That's easy," Sam said. "I want a napoleon."

"And you've known what to call them as long as I've known you."

"It's the only thing I remember about my mother," Samantha said quietly, and her emerald eyes darkened with wistfulness. "One afternoon, eating napoleons someplace far away."

"I didn't know you remembered her at all," Maggie said. "That's remarkable."

"When I remember that day, it's all golden around the edges. We must have been in a garden, because there were red flowers near my mother." She twisted a napkin. "And something I think of as a castle behind her."

"Probably England. I think you spent a lot of time there."

Sam nodded.

In light of the surprise Maggie had been exuberantly planning, the luncheon walk down memory lane could not have been better timed. She couldn't contain her excitement. She hurried Samantha through dessert, then outside toward a gallery several blocks down the street.

As they neared the gallery, Maggie spotted Sharon just climbing out of her car. The assistant editor/ photographer was dressed in one of the loose, belted dresses she preferred for assignments. Her braids were drawn back from her tan face into a crown topping her well-shaped head. Her dark eyes glittered as Sam and Maggie joined her, and she winked at Maggie.

"Boy," Sam commented, looking from one woman to the other, "you two would make terrible poker players." But her face showed that she, too, had caught the anticipation.

The glass-fronted gallery was two doors down, and as they approached it, Maggie watched her step-daughter's face. For a moment, there was a blank look as she took in the posters announcing the photographic display within. Then, as her gaze caught on a

large black-and-white likeness of the photographer,
her mouth dropped. She hurried forward to stare.

Maggie flashed a smile at Sharon.

Samantha whirled. "I look just like her, don't I?"

"You sure do, sweetie."

"Oh, thank you, Maggie," the girl said, flinging
herself into her stepmother's arms. "This is the best
surprise I've ever had."

"Well, silly, go on in. They have a wonderful ex-
hibit of your mother's work in there. You go ahead
and explore. Sharon and I are going to put together a
feature story for the paper this week."

With an enthusiastic kiss to Maggie's cheek, Sam
ran inside.

Sharon looked at the photo of Sarah Sven Henderson. "Samantha's her spitting image."

Maggie nodded. The photo had been taken, she
knew, by Paul Henderson in Ireland, just days before
Sarah's death. Sarah's long blond hair floated on a
breath of wind, and her expression was serious. "I
think it's wonderful that her work is being revived,"
Maggie commented. "She was one of the first women
news photographers to gain any attention. Have you
seen any of her work?"

Sharon shook her head. "I'm ashamed to admit
I've never had the opportunity."

"This is a double treat for you, then. Come on."

As Maggie and Samantha walked back to the car
two hours later, having left Sharon at her car, Sam was
pensive.

"Penny for your thoughts," Maggie offered softly.

Sam sighed. "I have a lot."

"I bet."

"I feel so...*shallow* when I look at her pictures. Like I'm just a conceited little girl for wanting to be a model."

"Everyone has something different to offer, Samantha. There's nothing wrong with wanting to model."

She shrugged. "Not very important, though, is it? I mean, there's all this stuff wrong with the world, and I want to be beautiful. That doesn't make me feel too great."

Maggie said nothing for a moment. "There's something to be said for beauty, Sam."

"Like what?" The question held deep skepticism.

"Relief, for one thing. Think about how relaxed you feel in a garden of beautiful roses, or the joy you feel when you look at a sunset."

Sam shrugged.

"Anyway," Maggie added, "there's plenty of time for you to decide." She linked an arm through Sam's. "Just keep an open mind. That's the important thing."

A shout startled Maggie from her quiet discussion just as they reached the car. She glanced over her shoulder. A half a block up, a small crowd had gathered in front of a record store, and Maggie glimpsed one of the silver-studded black leather jackets that so pointedly identified the speed rockers defending Proud Fox.

Instincts quivering, she turned to Samantha. "Grab the camera from the trunk," she said, throwing her the keys and scrambling for a notepad in her long pockets.

Sam moved quickly and joined Maggie as they hurried toward the crowd. The girl had been trained in the use of a camera at her father's knee, and she now checked the film count and settings, then slung the strap over her neck, focusing as they ran. In a moment, Maggie heard the whir of the camera motor as Sam snapped a few preliminary shots.

"How much film is there?" Maggie asked.

"Not much. About half a roll."

"I don't want you in the middle of this. Shoot from the edges of the crowd."

"Mother!" Sam protested. "How can I get anything decent from back there?"

With a mental kick, Maggie realized Samantha was burning with purpose. She bit her lip but made a split-second decision. "Do what you have to do," she said. "Just be careful."

She was rewarded with a solemn nod from Samantha, who kicked off her high heels near a doorway. Maggie noted the gesture and filed it.

As she reached the knot of curious onlookers, Maggie found two pairs of opposing soldiers in the ongoing war over rock and roll. Two boys, about fifteen, conservatively dressed, faced a couple of speed rockers in leather and long hair. A shouting match was going on.

Maggie forgot being a reporter, forgot her newspaper entirely. "What's going on here?" she shouted.

All four faces swiveled toward the authority in her voice. "Beat it, lady," said one of the rockers, his lip curling in a dismissive sneer. "This is none of your business."

"It is my business," she said, stepping forward. "You—" she glanced at each face in turn "—*all* of you, made it my business when your ridiculous fighting gave me seven stitches Wednesday."

"What are you, a teacher or something?" the same dark-haired boy asked. He was no more than sixteen, with the smooth jaw of one who has not yet seen a razor, but he was a solid six feet tall and exuded an attitude of sullen arrogance.

"No. I'm a reporter for the *Wanderer*." She addressed the entire group with crossed arms. "I've been following this story for two months, and frankly, I'm tired of it. Why don't you all back off and agree to live and let live?"

All four boys started talking at once, protesting her suggestion of détente with a dozen reasons why it couldn't work. No, Maggie realized, only three were protesting. The second speed rocker touched the arm of his friend, his blue eyes trained on Maggie. In those eyes, she saw the unmistakable glow of intelligence, and she addressed her next question to him. "Do you really think this is solving anything?"

Long blond lashes swept down to hide his expression. He said nothing.

"Are you going to quit buying records by Proud Fox?"

He frowned at her as though she'd just suggested a walk on Saturn.

"So what's the big deal?" she asked.

"They started it." He licked his lower lip, looking distinctly uncomfortable.

"I'm not finished yet," Maggie returned. She could feel the small crowd begin to disperse behind her, the thrill seekers bored with negotiation. She turned to the other boys, with their shorter hair. One even wore a tie. Maggie looked at the other one, who seemed more receptive. "Do you two think you're going to stop anyone from buying a record by protesting?"

The boy she had spoken to shifted uncomfortably, but the one with the tie spoke up. "That isn't the point. We believe Proud Fox is evil, and we won't stand for corruption anywhere in our society. We have a responsibility to protest the godless."

Maggie lost her tongue for a moment. "But if your actions are causing violence, isn't that evil, too?"

"We protest nonviolently. If others—" he glanced pointedly at the two rockers "—confront and incite violence, we cannot control that."

His cold delivery and the almost canned sound of his words bothered Maggie. Fifteen-year-olds didn't talk like that. She measured him silently for a moment. His lips were faintly twisted, a shape given them not by attitude but by an almost unnoticeable scar that ran from his lip to the corner of his eye.

Maggie saw it would be pointless to argue with him. "Why don't all of you pack it in for today?" she said with a sigh. "I'm sure there's something you could find to do with a Saturday afternoon."

The dark-haired rocker cocked his head at his friend. "Let's go." He threw a threatening glance toward the boy with the tie, but to Maggie's relief, they walked away.

The other two boys stood their ground, and with a shake of her head, Maggie turned to look for Samantha. For a moment, she didn't see her. Then a boy laughed and Maggie saw Samantha standing in the doorway where she had kicked off her shoes, talking to the tall blond rocker. His friend, the surly one, had walked on.

Sam's eyes were starry as she gazed at the boy, who tangled his fingers with hers. Sam dipped her head bashfully as he said something in a low voice, and then she darted a glance to his face, her expression clearly shouting her infatuation.

Maggie headed toward her daughter. Sam hastily straightened, dropping the boy's fingers. He nervously smoothed long, fine hair away from his face, the chains on his coat jangling.

"Mom," Samantha said, "I'd like you to meet David. David, this is my mother, Mrs. Henderson."

To Maggie's surprise, David extended his hand to shake hers shyly. "Pleased to meet you, Mrs. Henderson." He glanced down, then met her eyes squarely. "I'm sorry about that, back there."

"So am I," she said with some asperity.

"They're in the wrong, you know."

"Maybe." Maggie looked at Samantha. "It was nice to meet you, David, but as you've probably heard, Sam's on restriction for a week, and we have to go now."

He nodded and gave Samantha a long glance. "See ya at school," he said, touching her fingers as he passed.

"Okay," Sam murmured. She bent swiftly to retrieve her shoes and stomped toward the car. "You didn't have to be so rude," she lashed out as she reached the vehicle.

Maggie unlocked the doors without speaking, then met Sam's flashing eyes over the car. "I don't think I was rude, Samantha. You're overreacting."

"I bet you would have been nicer if we'd just run into him," Sam said, and flung herself into the car.

Maggie rolled her eyes and settled in next to her daughter. "Relax a little, sweetie."

Sam sighed. "I just like him so much," she said. "I want you to like him, too."

"Give me a chance. Two minutes on the street isn't enough time to learn much of anything."

The girl nodded. "Sorry."

"It's okay." Maggie started the car and pulled into traffic. Actually, David had been a pleasant surprise. Although first impressions could be deceiving, he seemed like a nice boy. Now his friend...

She let the thought go unfinished, unwilling to make judgments if she didn't have to. Samantha liked David and she had to trust her daughter's instincts for at least long enough to see what the boy was about.

Friday night, as Maggie brushed her teeth in preparation for bed, she reviewed the past week wearily. About the only purely good thing that had happened was the removal of the stitches in her eyebrow this morning. Examining the spot in the mirror, she thought it looked good. A little pink and puckered, but all in all, not bad.

The rest of the week, however, had left much to be desired. Samantha's moods had swung even more wildly than usual in response to her frustration at her restriction. One minute, she was the sweet, obedient child Maggie had raised, who did her chores without complaint. The next moment, she slumped from couch to kitchen to backyard, sulkily saying nothing.

In addition to the trouble on the home front, Maggie was swamped with work. Two members of her small staff had come down with colds, leaving Maggie, Sharon and three high-school interns to piece the paper together.

To further complicate matters, the newspaper offices had been flooded with letters about Proud Fox, both pro and con. Maggie had run an entire page of letters in this week's edition, along with an editorial she had written Saturday afternoon, urging peace.

Occasionally, she'd glimpsed Joel going or coming, and she often heard his movements through the walls. There had been little time in her week beyond the press of work and family, but his presence nagged her like a half-remembered song.

She had learned that he awakened in the morning to the sound of marches on the radio, at the same time she woke up. As she lay in her bed, steeling herself for the grim process of opening her eyes, she listened to those marches and imagined him jumping up and dressing to the blood-tingling notes of the drums and fifes. It led her to believe Joel Summer was a man of energy and movement.

Through the years, she'd grown used to the noises of neighbors in apartments and the oddly intimate knowledge one gained sharing walls with strangers. Like most people, she'd learned to shut all the distractions out, trusting others to do the same.

But she'd never had a neighbor like him. As she dabbed Vitamin E oil on the puckery scar on her eyebrow, she could hear him moving around just beyond the wall and tried to ignore it. When, a moment later, she heard his shower go on, Maggie felt her mouth go instantly dry. Not ten feet away, that perfectly formed body was dripping wet and bare. The knowledge sent a rush of heat through her middle, and for the most fleeting of seconds, she let herself imagine a torrid scene in which her body was pressed against his, their slippery, wet flesh sharing the running water.

Reality snatched the sultry vision away. She glimpsed her unadorned and decidedly unfeminine face in the mirror; her hair pulled back severely, the scar pink and angry over her eye. She shook her head in disgust at herself. Bad enough to have suddenly turned into a sneaky voyeur, ignoring the unwritten but precise rules of apartment living; she now had the nerve to contemplate passionate liaisons with a man who was definitely out of her class. She imagined Joel with a confident professional woman, a lawyer or doctor, perhaps—not an overly tall and less than graceful reporter.

She flicked the light off and hurried out of the bathroom. In the peaceful sanctuary of her bedroom, she shook her head, mortified. He wasn't a stripper or a photograph in a beefcake calendar, designed for ogling. It shamed her that she continued to think in that way about him—after all, hadn't women been complaining about it for years?

Assumptions, assumptions, assumptions, she thought as she climbed into bed and punched down her pillow. What did she really know about Joel Summer, anyway, except that he liked birds and ought to have considered a career as a movie star? A good reporter wouldn't be jumping to so many conclusions.

In the bedroom beyond the wall, she heard a sound. Covering her head, she groaned as another vision of him assailed her.

Maybe, she thought, it was impossible to completely eradicate the sensual part of one's nature. Maybe she was fighting too hard to ignore him. He was an undeniably handsome man, and beauty, as she'd told Samantha, was a very important part of life.

She settled in more comfortably, her mind somewhat eased. After all, she could never get enough of
the look of the first snow on the craggy summit of
Pikes Peak, but by January, she ceased to notice it at
all.

Chapter Four

Joel knelt at the foot of the lilac bushes Sunday morning, enjoying the early sunshine on his head and arms. The sweet smell of pungent earth rose to his nostrils as he dug a trench around the roots. But the mixture he poured into the prepared dugout smelled worse than a rotten egg.

"What *is* that?" asked a voice behind him. He turned to see Maggie, dressed in a simple green sundress and sandals, her hair caught back in a ponytail. The color set her golden eyes glimmering, as if small bits of light were trapped there.

He smiled. "Fish emulsion, powdered eggshells and water. Aromatic, isn't it?"

"That's an understatement." She wrinkled her nose. "Is it fertilizer or something?"

"Exactly." He lifted the bucket and moved to the next bush, cultivating the dirt around the roots with a forked hand tool. "It'll make these bushes bloom like you won't believe."

"You're a gardener, too?" Maggie folded her arms to calm the jitters she felt in his presence. She had seen him through the kitchen windows and had been unable to resist chatting with him for a few minutes.

He glanced at her over his shoulder, his eyes a brilliant, jeweled blue. "Man of many talents." He wet the earth with the last of the mixture and stood up. "I hope you don't mind, but it didn't look like anyone around here was serious about gardening."

She laughed. "Not hardly. I barely have time for myself, much less a hobby."

Wiping his hands on a clean cloth at his belt, he said, "Do you have a few minutes for a cup of coffee?" He grinned, showing off that single, searing dimple. "I have someone I'd like you to meet."

"The old tom?" Maggie asked, delighted.

"Good guess."

"I had faith you could do it."

"Come on, then. I'll give you a proper introduction."

She followed him across the grass, trying not to notice how the worn-white jeans hugged his broad thighs. Then, remembering the path of least resistance that would—hopefully—help her overcome this ridiculous infatuation, she allowed herself an appreciative appraisal of his back beneath a cotton tank.

At his door, he stepped aside to let her go ahead. "Watch out in there. I ordinarily don't have people in through the back door."

As her eyes adjusted, Maggie saw fifty-five gallon drums neatly arranged around the small, enclosed back porch. "Is this the recycling center?" she asked with a smile.

He inclined his head a little ruefully. "You're lucky you're seeing it when I've just started over in a new house. It's not usually a very neat area."

Maggie looked at him. "Neatness isn't really the point, though, is it?"

He smiled. "No, it isn't." For a brief second, his eyes caught hers in a gentle appraisal. He gestured toward the kitchen. "In here."

The earthy scent of freshly brewed coffee welcomed her, and she breathed the aroma thankfully, glancing around curiously. He had either accumulated very little in the way of decorations, or he had not yet had time to put them up in the kitchen, for the walls were bare and only a single plant grew in the curtainless window. The floor, however, gleamed with a recent mopping, and his dishes had been put away.

"So, would you like a cup of coffee?" he asked, washing his hands.

"If it tastes as good as it smells, I'll arm wrestle you for the pot."

"It does, but I'll share." He filled two heavy ceramic mugs with the dark brew. "Cream or sugar?"

"All of the above. Please."

He smiled, taking down containers of each. "Me, too. My mom raised us on a mixture of half coffee, half milk—I still drink it in almost the same combination."

His hands dwarfed the mug, the spoon looking like a miniature between long, graceful fingers. They were hands accustomed to work by the look of the nicks and scratches marring their backs, but for their size, they were deft and nimble.

She sipped the aromatic coffee and exclaimed, "Wow!"

"Jamaica Blue Mountain. The best coffee in the world. A professor of mine used to drink it."

"It really is fantastic. Thanks."

"My pleasure." Gesturing, he added, "I think the cat is probably still asleep on the couch."

At the thought of going with him into the front room, Maggie felt her tension return. The kitchen was safe somehow, not as comfortable. Grow up, Maggie. Adults do sometimes have conversations in places other than kitchens.

After the barren aura of the back of the house, the living room was a surprise. It was welcoming, designed for relaxing and reading and quiet conversation. Curled in a corner of the couch, looking considerably cleaner than Maggie had ever seen him, was the old tom.

"Wake up, you old lazy," Joel growled, scooping the cat into his arms. There were still knots in the cat's fur, and one ear drooped sadly. He meowed softly at

Joel, who turned to Maggie. "Meet Moses Many-Toes."

She gave him a puzzled smile. "Many-Toes?"

"Look." He tugged one of the cat's paws, and Moses let it dangle in Joel's hand like a lady awaiting a kiss from a count. Beyond the normal five claws and pads, this cat had three more that jutted out like a big thumb, giving his paw the appearance of a hand.

"He could practically toss a baseball," she commented dryly. "Will he bolt if I pet him?"

"I don't think so—just go easy. He doesn't have much trust to spare."

Gingerly, Maggie stretched her fingers forward for the cat to smell. When he seemed to accept her, she rubbed his blunt, broad head, carefully skirting the ear. "Why, he's as soft as down," she said with wonder. "You're a good old cat, aren't you?" The cat's eyes blinked lazily, and a rusty purr sounded in the quiet room.

Touched that he had found refuge after so long a time of suffering, Maggie looked up at Joel to find him watching her closely. "You're an unusual man, Joel."

He made a depreciative noise. "So I've been told." He turned to settle the cat back into his corner. "Have a seat," he invited, taking one of the chairs by the window.

Maggie followed suit. A deep and pregnant pause fell between them, and after enduring it for a moment, casting around for something to say, she risked a glance at him. At the same moment, he turned to look at her. With a ripple of intuition, Maggie finally understood that he was nearly as nervous as she. Impulsively, she grinned. "You know, I hear your marches in the morning."

"Do you?" He straightened. "I should turn them down, then."

"No, please don't. It's part of sharing walls. You're a hundred times more polite than a great many of the neighbors I've had over the years." She sipped her coffee. "I'm sure you hear us, too."

He grinned. "MTV when you're gone."

Maggie laughed. "Samantha turns it on to do her housework. Does she play it too loud?"

"No, not at all." He glanced at Maggie and smiled. "I mean, it's *loud*, but I can live with it. She's just a kid."

"That's kind of you. Not everyone is patient with children."

"I like kids."

"Do you have any of your own?"

"No." For a brief span, a sadness flitted over his face. "No," he repeated, "things didn't work that way for me."

"You sound like you've lost your only chance. You must be what? Thirty-five? Men have fathered nations at sixty."

He half shrugged. "We'll see."

Maggie glanced at him, at the sudden distance reflected in his eyes, and she felt again that there was something in his past that gave him pain. She sipped her coffee.

As if uncomfortable with the turn in the conversation, he asked, "Where's Samantha today?"

"She goes to church with my grandmother. I go to the eight o'clock service, but Samantha refuses to get up that early on a weekend morning. They usually have lunch and spend the afternoon together."

"I've seen your grandmother," he said. "The elegant lady?"

Maggie nodded with a grin. "That's her."

"Is that where you get that Texas sound in your voice?"

"I didn't know I had one." Maggie frowned quizzically. "Do I?"

"A little bit—just a word here and there. I heard it when you talked to the cat."

Maggie laughed. "They tell me I had a right proper slur until I went to school. And I've never even visited Texas—isn't that strange?"

"Was your grandmother around?"

"Yes." With a barely audible sigh, a reflexive gesture linked to any mention of her childhood, she said, "My father was stationed at Fort Carson until I was seven. My mother doesn't have a drawl anymore, but she must have when I was a child—they'd only been in Colorado for a year or so when my parents got married."

"Are you an army brat?"

"Yes," she said, immediately defensive.

"I would never have guessed."

"Is there something you look for? A mark on the forehead or something?"

Joel grinned. "I didn't mean it like that—army kids always made me feel like the biggest hick in the world."

"Really? Why?"

"Your living rooms had things from Germany and Europe and Okinawa." He laughed, meeting her gaze briefly before glancing toward the cat stretching and resettling on the couch. "You all had braces when you needed them and had seen dozens of places that were just names on a map to me."

Maggie laughed in sympathy. "And I envied the natives of whatever city we were living in with a spirit bordering on hatred. You all had friends you'd known since kindergarten, and you didn't have to start school in a new place all the time or live with the prejudice some entire towns hold against the military."

He lifted his coffee cup in a mock toast. "To shattered misconceptions," he said.

Maggie grinned and touched his cup. "Did you grow up here, Joel?"

He nodded, looking into his cup. "It's been a long time since I've lived here. I left to go to college and didn't come back until eight months ago."

"Where'd you go to school?"

"Colorado State and Cornell."

"Cornell? Well, now," she said with a teasing lilt to her words, "I had no idea I was in the company of such a nimble brain."

Joel laughed—a rich, earthy sound. "I'm no smarter than the next guy. Just dedicated. Like a pit bull."

Maggie looked at him. He was undoubtedly dedicated, but the brains were there, too.

Another still pause fell between them, a space of moments Maggie filled by letting her gaze wander around his living room. Predictably, the books on the shelves leaned toward the natural sciences, and there was a huge collection of titles on birds. But there were other books, as well—Longfellow and Wordsworth, a cross section of modern paperbacks and a handful of the kinds of books required for a college English credit.

On the walls hung a distinctive selection of framed photographs: a trio of hawks at dawn; an empty beach; a single, watering deer. They were lonely photos. She wondered silently if he had taken them.

"So, Maggie," he said, breaking her reverie, "I was planning to go out in a little while, go up to the mountains. Would you like to come along?"

Such a straightforward invitation, she thought, biting her lip—but spending time with him wasn't the way to overcome her crush. Even now, as he waited calmly for her answer, he exuded an astonishing level of sexual appeal. Was it his eyes? His shoulders? His wide mouth?

Joel tried to maintain a poised facade, but he felt Maggie's intense perusal. When her pale brown eyes tangled with his, he was surprised by the sultriness in them. For a moment, he let himself meet that fire, feeling his breath fill his chest with hot pressure, but when his imagination provided him with a vision of her, tawny and tigerlike beneath him, he inhaled slowly. "What do you say?" he asked.

His rough voice rolled all the way down her spine, pooling with velvet vibration in her lower back. "Yes," she said. "I'd like that."

"Good." He stood up. "Why don't we change clothes and meet outside in twenty minutes?"

"Okay." She rose to her feet, too, and was struck again with the delight of having a man standing so much taller than her—it was a distinct pleasure to feel small for a change. She felt a primitive security in his size.

With a start, she realized she'd been staring far too long into his jeweled eyes. "I'll meet you on the porch," she said hastily.

At home, she changed quickly into a T-shirt and jeans, straightened up the house and left a note for Samantha. As she secured her front door behind her, she saw Joel lowering a pack into the back of his truck. He'd exchanged his tank top for a long-sleeved cotton shirt that did nothing to hide his powerful physique. They weren't the muscles of a weight lifter, bunchy and obvious. Rather, Maggie thought, they were like the sleek, healthy configurations of a stallion. There was nothing she could do to prevent the recurring visions she had of running her palms over him. All over him. The thought made her grin to herself.

"Ready?" he said, lifting his heavy, dark brows.

Maggie smoothed her grin away with the tips of her fingers. "Sure."

"Do you mind if I play some blues?" he asked as he settled next to her in the cab of the pickup.

"Not at all."

He pushed a waiting cassette into the tape deck, and the mellow southern cords of Sonny and Brownie filled the cab.

"I have a brother who's a blues fanatic," Maggie commented.

"Does he live around here, too?" Joel asked as he maneuvered the truck onto the road.

"Oh, no you don't," Maggie said. "I've been talking about myself nonstop." She brushed a lock of hair out of her eyes. "Your turn. I know you like the blues and animals and that you're as smart as a whip."

"See, there it is," he said, throwing a dazzling glance at her. "That drawl—'lahk the blues.'"

"Not fair," she replied, refusing to be distracted. She needed to know more of him, needed to find some way to get a handle on who he was, exactly. "How many children in your family?"

"Four. Three girls and me."

"You must have been spoiled rotten."

Joel smiled, eyes on the road. "I'm also the youngest."

"Hmm," Maggie said, cocking her head. "Now I'm surprised."

"Why?"

"I don't know."

"Because," he said, his face suddenly serious, "you'd expect me to be a little more open, right?"

Startled at the insight, she stared at him. Grim tension gripped his jaw. "Exactly," she said finally.

His throat moved as he swallowed, and he carefully negotiated a turn, heading west. When he spoke, each word was carefully enunciated. "I had a really rotten marriage." At a traffic light, he braked and looked at Maggie. "Since then, I haven't spent much time with women."

In his eyes, she caught an undiluted glimpse of raw emotion—pain and hunger, sorrow and entreaty. In that moment, she felt an inexplicable link spring up between them, a link far beyond infatuation or attraction. It was almost, she thought, as if she had suddenly climbed inside him and he in her, without touching at all.

A horn honked behind them, and Joel released the brake. He looked out the windshield. "Have you spent much time up Rampart Range road?" His voice showed nothing.

Maggie tried to match his tone. "Not really," she answered. She rubbed her palms together, staring out the window. The rhythm of her heart had nothing to do with the giddiness she had been feeling. It was terror, plain and simple. If he decided to draw her in, keeping this man at arm's length would be no easy feat.

As she watched the buildings grow sparse, the trees thick, she realized she had discovered the first flaw in her newly created sincere men category. Intensity. Yes, she thought, stealing a glance at his profile, that should have been obvious. A man couldn't very well be sincere without something motivating it. A certain amount of passion would be required.

She'd spent her life avoiding the emotional highs and lows that had proved so disastrous for her parents. Passion about anything was dangerous, a theory reinforced by the pain that had been reflected in Joel's eyes.

The farther they moved from the city, the more relaxed he became. By the time they reached the destination he had picked out, Maggie could sense a new man emerging, one more in line with the youngest child and only son in a family of daughters.

"Do you like to hike?" he asked.

"Depends on how difficult a hike it turns out to be," she countered. "I wouldn't be thrilled to have to cling to the edge of a cliff, for example."

She was rewarded with a grin. "I wouldn't do that to you." He slung a nylon backpack over one shoulder, then easily took her hand as they walked through a wide clearing of pale green grass. "I did it to my cousins from Jersey once, though."

"What did you do?"

"I took them on the hardest hike of their lives." His voice lifted with remembered mischief. "Right along the edge of a sandstone cliff over a drop of about twelve or fifteen hundred feet."

"Oh, Lord," she breathed, dizzy at the very thought. "I, for one, would have lost my breakfast."

"And you wouldn't have been alone," he said, tongue-in-cheek. "They promised me their combined allowances for the next ten years if I would get them down."

"Why did you do it?"

He swung her hand. "They always laughed about the Springs. I was jealous of them going into New York City to shop the same way I was jealous of all you army kids." He laughed. "God paid me back, though."

Maggie smiled. "Pray tell."

He winced appreciatively. "I broke my ankle on the way down."

"That's perfect."

"My cousins had to carry me back to the car, and while they went swimming and rode bikes and took part in all the wonders of summer, I hobbled around on crutches."

"Oh, no."

"It gets worse. My father whipped me good for taking them up there, giving my cousins even more to rib me about."

"Was it worth it?"

Joel stopped, facing her for a brief moment. Then his clear eyes moved to scan the sky with familiarity and fondness. "When we reached the summit of the cliff, we startled a red-tailed hawk. He was a beauty, too, half as big as we were, perched on the tip of a rock out in the middle of nothing. He flew up, right above us, and it seemed like he hung there forever." Joel had been outlining his words with his free hand as he spoke. Now he dropped it and looked at Maggie with a half smile. "I fell head over heels in love with that bird. I'd do the whole day over again in a second."

As she looked at him, Maggie felt a swoosh of reaction within her, and she wanted to press a hand to the concrete manifestation of joy on his features. She didn't dare. "Is there a chance we could see a big bird like that up here now?" she asked.

"Always. This is their country." He inclined his head. "Come on. I'll show you a great spot."

He led her through a stand of coniferous trees, up the mountain for quite a distance. By the time they reached a tumble of pink granite boulders, Maggie was unabashedly breathing hard. Joel, however, settled comfortably on a speckled rock with no more sign of exertion than if he'd walked across their porch at home.

When she could breathe without gasping, she said, "I've got a feeling you're one of those disgustingly healthy types who eats nothing but bean sprouts and runs marathons for the fun of it." She collapsed on the ground, hearing him laugh.

"Not hardly." He tugged a shaft of grass from its sheath and playfully reached over to tickle her face with it. "I was born to hike trails and till fields and break horses. I don't expect everyone to be strong— it's easy for me."

"I'm not exactly a shrimp," she muttered. But she was recovering more quickly than she'd believed possible, and in the wake of her gasps there came an exhilarated tingling to her veins.

"No, you're not," he agreed, smiling. "You were born for it, too. You just don't know it yet."

"How would you know?"

He laughed with a freedom Maggie would have said was impossible two hours before. "Look at yourself, woman. You're as strong as an ox."

Maggie frowned at him. "Thanks a lot."

He moved to sit beside her on the grass. "That's not what I meant," he said in his gravelly voice. Gently, he lifted a hand to touch her cheek. "I really think you look like a tiger."

At the warmth of his long fingers against her face, Maggie felt her heart flip oddly. It was a delight to simply stare into his eyes, she thought, to examine so closely the texture of his skin. He smelled like sun-dried clothes and warm earth, a faintly musky, pleasant scent. "I think you look like a redwood tree," she offered in return.

"That's new." He touched her hair with the very tips of his fingers, following the gesture with his eyes. Slowly, he shifted his gaze back to her face. "I haven't let myself like a woman for a long time, Maggie," he said softly. "I might be a little rusty." She felt his knuckles skirt the edge of her jaw. "You tell me if I'm breaking the rules."

"I don't think I've personally had enough practice to know the rules," she said. "I don't think we've broken any so far."

"Good." For another moment, he measured her seriously, then took her hand and helped to her feet. "Let's go up a little higher."

The climb from the boulders up the mountain was not as steep as the first leg of the hike had been, and Maggie felt a sense of solid well-being invade her. Overhead, in a sky so deep and blue that it defied description, the sun shone brilliantly. Blue spruce and ponderosa pine trees rustled with the breeze. Birds and small animals scurried away from the humans in their realm, and Maggie caught sight of a tiny bluebird high in an aspen.

Just ahead of her, Joel walked with deceptive ease, his hair glinting in the sun like a broken bit of volcanic rock that still glowed with ancient, reddish heat.

He led them to a field near the summit of the mountain, a wide field fronted with trees. A great drop into nothingness edged the other side. As she followed him into the tall grass dotted with wildflowers, Maggie looked around her in exuberance.

For, beyond the safe bowl in which they stood, the mountains stretched endlessly, furry and blue in places; hazy and golden in others. "This is beautiful," Maggie whispered in awe.

Joel grinned broadly. "My favorite spot on earth."

A magpie flew over, flashing black-and-white feathers, uttering a harsh, but somehow cheerful, call. When it had passed, there was no other sound.

Or perhaps there was, Maggie thought, listening. A plethora of bird sounds emanated from the trees; an insect burred, the wind moaned through the valley below.

Joel squatted and unzipped his backpack, drawing out a long package wrapped in plastic and a ball of string. He shot Maggie a look of pure mischief. "Are you any good with kites?"

"Not really. Mine always take uncontrollable nose-dives."

He opened the package and unrolled a kite shaped like a bird in flight. With the kind of efficiency born of practice, he spread it out and began fitting stickers to prepunched holes.

She watched as he finished the assembly, then threaded light string through the breast of the bird printed on the kite. "Here we go," he said, standing. "There are some cans of pop in my pack, if you're thirsty. Help yourself."

"Thanks." Her mouth was as dry as dust, and she found a cola, settling in the grass to watch Joel. It didn't take long to get the kite up, and he reeled it out into the deep sky, tugging at the string at critical moments, backing up and dashing forward until it drifted high above the earth.

He backed up, pulling the kite with him, until he stood next to Maggie. "Here, you try it."

He held out a hand to help her to her feet and put the spool in her hands. "When it pulls hard, give it some line. When it starts to dip or lose altitude, reel it in."

Nervously, Maggie accepted the responsibility. When, after a few minutes, the kite showed no danger of suddenly plummeting to the ground, she relaxed and began to enjoy the rhythmic pull on the string.

Joel fished an apple out of his pack, backing away to let Maggie handle the kite on her own. As he sat down on the ground, he could see the exact moment she lost her nervousness and began to enjoy herself; her stance relaxed and she shook loosened tendrils of hair away from her exotic face.

The apple was mealy but sweet. Joel savored it as he filled his eyes with her. Her T-shirt clung lightly to uplifted breasts and a slender waist. The jeans were just tight enough to outline a generous bottom and long legs, and her skin showed a hint of rosy dampness from the walk. As he absorbed her, she laughed at some inner thrill of accomplishment, and her jewelry glinted at her wrists and ears.

She was impossible to resist. Her vibrant good nature was a balm to his weary spirit, giving him a sense of warmth he had not known in many, many years.

Beyond that, there was an innocent sensuality about her that told Joel she'd never really explored that portion of herself, no matter how long she'd been married. The sultriness in her eyes hinted at the tiger lurking beneath her innocence, and he couldn't stop wondering what it would be like to set the tiger free.

Enough, his aroused body cautioned. In accordance with its warning, Joel tossed the apple core into the trees for forest creatures and stood up to share the kite.

Heavy clouds rolled in toward midafternoon, forcing Joel and Maggie to reel in the kite and get back down the mountain. In the truck, he said, "I'm famished. Would you like to stop for something to eat in Manitou? Do you have time?''

"Are you kidding?" Maggie returned. "If I don't get food pretty soon, I'll eat the dashboard." She sighed, touching her stomach.

"Great."

"I'll buy lunch, since you've so generously introduced me to such a glorious place."

He grinned. "Fair enough, I guess."

They drove into Manitou Springs, the somewhat Bohemian sister city that joined the western edges of Colorado Springs. Over sandwiches and huge glasses of iced tea, they laughed and talked as easily as childhood friends, a fact Maggie didn't even notice until they were nearly finished.

After lunch, Joel led her into a games arcade that was built over the stream that ran out of the mountains and through Manitou. Shops stocked with scenic photographs and souvenirs of Pikes Peak for the coming tourist rush lined the labyrinthian open-air mall. Laughter spilled out of a skeeball parlor.

"When I was little," Joel said, "my dad used to bring me here at night." He paused on the wooden slats and looked down to the creek running below, its water giving a rushing, echoey undertone to the sound of the bells and buzzers on the games. "It used to scare me to death to walk on these boards in the dark and know I could fall all the way down there." He grinned. "I never let go of his hand."

As she stared at the quicksilver water visible between the boards, Maggie touched her forehead and blinked, imagining what it would be like here at night, with red and blue neon flashing and crowds pushing around her.

Joel chuckled. "Gets to you, doesn't it?"

As she was about to answer, a great crack of lightning split the sky, followed almost instantly by a resounding rumble of thunder. Maggie started violently and clapped her hands to her ears. "Looks like we're going to get our storm early today," she shouted.

He touched her arm. "Do you want to make a run for the truck or duck into a doorway?"

The question was settled as another bolt of electricity split the sky with pink light. Maggie and Joel ran for an archway a few feet away, cringing as thunder cracked again. Joel pointed to a park bench nestled under a stone roof, and they ran to reach it between the cracks.

Maggie's hands were shaking as she sat down. The coppery odor of raw wattage hung in the air, and the hairs on her arms stood up. "Did you know," she said in the most conversational voice she could muster, "that more people die of lightning in Colorado than in almost any other state in the country?"

"Does it scare you?"

"Not if I'm safely inside." A small ribbon of nervous laughter spun from her throat.

Joel smiled and started to slip an arm around her shoulders. As he touched her, a current of static electricity spit between them. He laughed. "Sparks are flying."

And not only those in nature, she thought as he wrapped his arm around her fully, pulling her closer to him. She bit her lip at the sudden flush of awareness jumping to life all over her body. She fixed her eyes on the dazzling sky.

Joel watched the storm play on her eyes, his nerves trained on her reactions to him. At his touch, she'd gone taut, but she didn't resist him.

Her earlobe, hung with a silver-and-coral earring that matched her heavy bracelet, peeked out from below her hair. Joel touched it with his fingers, tracing the curved edge, then moved down to the angle of her jaw, where he brushed the invisible hair protecting her skin.

He'd forgotten how soft a woman's skin felt. He traced the edge of her face to her chin, drinking in the symmetrical slants, and Maggie sat poised, as unmoving as a doll. Under his arm, the muscles of her shoulders began to relax.

With infinite patience, he turned her face to his and waited until she looked at him. Her eyes fluttered closed as he let himself move forward to touch his lips to hers.

The storm went silent behind them, or, Joel thought, he simply couldn't hear it through the rush of noise in his ears. It wasn't just the static hanging in the air that stung his lips and lifted the hair on his neck, either. It was her lips, tasting of the sugar she'd put in her tea; lips infinitely succulent and warm.

A sample was all he'd intended to take, but in his soft exploration, he drifted. He felt the pale heat of her hand as it fell on his shoulder and the shift in her body as she eased ever so slightly into him. Her mouth opened in invitation, and he joyfully met the opening.

At the first blazing touch of their tongues, Maggie gasped and Joel with her. For one aching second, both hesitated, but as thunder cracked again overhead with a violent, sky-shattering noise, they were lost.

Joel grabbed her close to him, pressing them together as he gave himself up to the maelstrom that had been hovering all day. He buried his hands in her hair, feeling his chin bump hers hard, their kiss so deep he could barely breathe.

He was losing control and he knew it. In a moment, he'd be tearing away her dress to taste the soft roundness of her breasts.

With his hands on either side of her head, he quieted their joining with slower and slower movements. "I knew you were in there," he whispered, swallowing when her darkened eyes, limpid with passion, met his.

"I don't think I was your maiden aunt, after all, Captain," she said with a smile.

He grinned and glanced over her shoulder. "The coast is clear on your side. Is there a crowd behind me?"

"I think we're safe." She relaxed her hold, a brittle trembling lingering in her fingers as the full impact of his kiss settled into her brain. "I guess it's a little late for a blush," she said, her eyes focused upon the hard rain falling now just beyond their enclave.

"Trust your instincts, Maggie."

She looked at him. His dark hair was disheveled, his shirt rumpled at the shoulders. The moment could have been awkward, but there was something so comfortable about him that the sudden, explosive intensity of their kiss seemed the most natural thing in the world.

He smoothed a wisp of her hair away from her face. "I haven't kissed anyone in a very long time, not like that." His voice rumbled almost below register. "I didn't mean to get so carried away."

Did that mean he would have kissed anyone that way? Maggie looked at her hands, creeping nervousness easing in behind her passion. She knew *she* wouldn't have responded like that to just anyone. No man had ever smelled and tasted so exquisitely perfect.

As if he sensed the direction of her thoughts, Joel lifted her hand and pressed the back of it to his cheek. "There's something very special about you, Maggie. Maybe about us. Don't fight it."

She wanted to believe him, wanted to believe this strong and gentle man was what he seemed to be, but the power of her own reactions told her it was just too dangerous to give him that much of herself—not yet. "Passion—desire—isn't all that uncommon," she said, drawing her hand back. "And I have a fifteen-year-old daughter. I have to be a good example."

"What are we doing that would be a bad example? Sharing an afternoon? Kissing in the storm?" He sighed. "Whatever you're afraid of, I wouldn't have torn away your clothes and taken you on the bench."

It wasn't, Maggie thought darkly, that she was afraid of what they had been doing. The problem lay more with what she'd wanted them to be doing, but a team of a hundred horses couldn't have dragged that admission from her. "Frankly," she continued, "it doesn't seem wise to get mixed up with a next-door neighbor," Maggie continued. "If we end up hating each other, life could get pretty uncomfortable."

He laughed. "I'll move if that happens," he said. "I promise." With a boyish grin, he nudged her with an elbow. "We'll take it as slow as you need to go, okay?"

How was she supposed to resist those dazzling blue eyes, those impish dimples? Almost against her will, she smiled in return. "Okay."

"Now," he said, settling comfortably against the back of the bench, his arms spread to either side of him, his legs stretched out in front of him, "tell me about Samantha. You don't seem old enough to have a teenager."

"No. I married her father when I was nineteen. Sam was five. Her mother had died." She paused, remembering the long, lonely years of her marriage. "Partly he married me so that she could have a mother, and that part worked out pretty well. He's always traveled constantly, and when we got divorced, it was natural that Samantha continue to live with me, so that she'd have some stability in her life."

"Does she still see him?"

Amiably, Maggie nodded. "She'll spend six weeks with him as soon as school is out, and whenever he blows into Denver for a while, she visits him. They have a good relationship, even if it is a little different."

"You love her."

"She's my daughter," Maggie said simply.

Joel seemed to absorb this for a while, then asked, "Are you ever jealous of her natural mother?"

"Not at all." She told him about the photographic display she had taken Samantha to the week before. "All week Samantha's been shooting film of everything from wooden spoons to the lace on the curtains. It thrilled her when I ran one of the photos she took in the *Wanderer*."

"That's great. Does she have any talent?"

"Naturally I think she does." Maggie smiled. "If you want an objective opinion, you'll have to ask someone else."

The rain trickled off suddenly, then stopped. "Well, that's it for the rain today," Joel said.

"We should get back," Maggie said. "Samantha will be wondering where I am."

He nodded and stood up, extending a hand to Maggie. When she stood, he didn't move for a moment, then brushed her hair from her face gently. "I had a nice time with you today, Maggie." He paused, his eyes lazily touching each section of her face. "I'd like to see you again."

Carried away by his nearness, enveloped by his natural scent and the power of his eyes, Maggie simply nodded.

It wasn't until later, with her hands in sudsy dishwater after dinner, that the spell he'd cast wore off sufficiently for Maggie to realize she still knew next to nothing about Joel Summer. Which meant she still didn't have a way to manage him, classify him.

There was nothing that made her more nervous.

Chapter Five

Although there had been several demonstrations at record stores around the city through the week, none of them had resulted in violence, and Maggie had chosen to ignore the entire problem in that week's paper. Mail had trickled off, and what seemed to be happening was that the speed rockers were ignoring demonstrations.

Friday morning, Maggie was finally free to concentrate on an edition with some fun—the end-of-school celebration. It was always one of the biggest issues of the year, highlighting fashions and entertainment. She would run the list of concerts for the summer and pinpoint the best upcoming movies. "Sharon," she called across the newsroom, where her photographer/assistant editor was blocking out a page with blue pencil. "Where are the concert lists?"

Sharon straightened, sticking her pencil into the braids swept to the top of her head. "I saw them come in but haven't had a chance to look them over." She riffled through a stack of mail. "Here they are." She also withdrew a long white envelope. "You have a letter here from Mitchell, did you know that?"

"It took him long enough." Mitchell was Maggie's longtime pen pal, a liaison established when Maggie's brother had been in prison. Galen's sentence had been a short one, but his friend Mitchell had not been so lucky. Maggie had been writing him for almost seven years.

Sharon passed over the sheaf of concert appearances and the thick letter from Mitchell. His envelopes were distinctive, always decorated with exquisite, tiny drawings—forest scenes and oceanside gatherings without people, only creatures of earth and sea and sky. Today's envelope showed a bright yellow butterfly with spots of blue on its wings, floating on a current of wind. A rise of mountains gave the address, which was written in Mitchell's extraordinary hand, its background. In flowing script at the bottom of the drawing was written, "The Great Spirit, the Creator, Flashing light through all the heaven...."

"If you ever get tired of writing that guy," Sharon said, looking over Maggie's shoulder, "pass him on to me. Every time one of his letters comes here, it's like a sunrise." She frowned at the lines written below the drawing. "A man who quotes Longfellow is the man for me."

"Did you have to memorize *The Song of Hiawatha*?" Maggie asked with a smile. "'By the shore of Gitchegoumee...'" She put the letter away in her jacket pocket to enjoy later. "Sam read it recently."

"How's it going with her new boyfriend, by the way?"

Maggie shook her head. "We're talking love here. Since Sam's restriction was lifted Monday, he's called every day and he walks her home from the bus stop." She smiled. "It's kind of sweet."

"Is he nice?"

"As a matter of fact, he seems like a pretty good kid." She paused. David seemed to really care about Sam, showing a tenderness that was rare for so young a boy. "He has nice manners and he works like thirty hours a week as a busboy and dishwasher at Denny's."

"Shows initiative," Sharon said with approval.

"I agree." She looked at her friend ruefully. "It's just so sudden," she said.

"And she's your baby."

Maggie nodded. "And she's my baby," she echoed. It was still a surprise to Maggie that she'd had any reservations at all about any teenager on the sole basis of his appearance. But she had. With a bitter twist of her lips, she said, "You know, my dad was such a fanatic about long hair that he used to beat my brother constantly about his hair. He finally wrestled Galen down in the kitchen and hacked it all off with a pair of sewing scissors."

Sharon shook her head in sympathy.

"That was when he ran away. Didn't see him again for five years."

"And now he's working in one of the roughest detention centers in New Mexico, trying to work miracles with kids who've got nothing left to lose," Sharon said. "That means something."

Maggie took a breath. "I think Samantha's David reminds me of Galen." Shaking her head, she pushed her reading glasses up on her nose to examine the concert schedules. "Good music at Redrocks this year," she commented, "though I doubt the kids will think so. Maybe you and I can catch a concert or two."

With her usual grace, Sharon let the previous subject of conversation slide away unnoticed. "We say that every summer."

"I know, but aren't you tired of the same old things going on all the time?"

"Sure I am." She settled herself comfortably on the edge of Maggie's desk. "But a concert—" She broke off with a shrug. "What I'd love is a trip to Jamaica and a mad encounter with somebody who whispers sweet nothings in my ear."

Maggie grinned, leaning her chin on her fist. "Mmm," she murmured, imagining a tropical breeze on her face, the smell of salt water heavy in the air. "Go on."

"Or," Sharon murmured in a barely audible voice, thick with appreciation, "I'd take this coming in the door right now."

Maggie glanced up to see Joel filling the doorway, an enigmatic smile gracing his dark face. "Joel!" she said, and stood up, knocking three pens to the floor in the process. "What brings you here?"

"I happened to be in the neighborhood and thought you might like to have some lunch." His smile stretched into a grin. "I have it on good authority that you're pretty fond of burgers."

He looked so good, Maggie thought. She liked the ease with which he carried his body, the casual comfort he seemed to feel in any situation. "I'd love to. Sharon, would you like to join us?"

A sparkle in Sharon's almond-shaped eyes gleamed as she answered. "Oh, no, you guys run along."

"Okay, then." Maggie took off her glasses with an effort to appear poised and slipped her light jacket over her shoulders.

As she and Joel were about to depart, Sharon spoke up. "Uh, Maggie, I just saw this," she said, waving one of the concert lists. "Guess who's going to be in Colorado Springs the end of next month?"

Maggie sighed and unconsciously touched the scar dividing her left eyebrow. "Proud Fox."

Sharon lifted her chin in confirmation. "Run it or not?"

"We don't have much choice, ethically."

The assistant editor nodded. "You got it."

* * *

Outside, Joel took her hand. "I missed you this week," he said, giving her fingers a squeeze.

"I've been working hard."

"Me, too." At his truck, he opened the door for her, then went around and got inside. A breeze carried his nearly oriental after-shave to her nostrils, a scent as exotic and mysterious as the man himself. "I'm going to drive to a very public place, and we'll eat our lunch in the company of lots of other people, but before I get there, I'd like one small kiss," he said as he took her face in his hands. He kissed her quickly, then once more, slowly, when she didn't protest.

His lips were what she remembered, sensual and firm; his wide mouth a generous terrain she wanted to explore. She swallowed as he pulled away to start the engine. "Today, it's your turn," she said.

"My turn for what?"

"To talk about yourself."

"All right," he agreed, pulling into traffic. "Where shall I start?"

With your secrets, she thought. Aloud, she said, "Tell me about your wife."

He shot a glance at her. "Don't mince words, Maggie," he said with a hint of sarcasm. "Just jump in anywhere."

"Sorry." She winced in apology. "I'm not known for my tact."

For a moment, he was silent, then he licked his lower lip quickly. "And I take myself too seriously most of the time." He smiled suddenly.

Maggie grinned, relieved that he hadn't taken offense.

"I met Nina in high school," he said. "We got married when we graduated, and she followed me all over the country while I went to school." He shifted gears and pulled around a slow-moving bus. "She ended up costing me everything."

Maggie remembered his admission that he'd not kissed anyone in a long time. That, coupled with the fleeting bitterness that flooded his eyes in unguarded moments, told her that one of the things his wife had cost him was his heart.

"I lost my trust with Paul," she volunteered suddenly. "It's been very hard for me to trust men since our marriage."

"Did he—" Joel asked, floundering for a polite way to ask the question.

Maggie laughed without bitterness. "Yes," she filled in for him. "He had a woman in every port, and I didn't know for a long time."

"That was Nina," he said. "The thing that killed me later was that my friends all knew. I felt like such a fool."

"I felt like that at first. Then I decided to just let it all go."

"Except that you can't trust anyone."

Maggie nodded as they turned into the parking lot of a hamburger stand. Joel shut off the engine and paused. "Well, maybe we both get another chance."

She met his serious look. "Maybe," she said, lifting one shoulder.

The crowds that gathered for lunch made further conversation impossible until they had ordered and found a table. Over a sloppy double cheeseburger, fries and a large soft drink, Maggie asked him about his sisters, his parents, his childhood. His replies painted a portrait of a warm, working-class background, where books and conversation were placed at a high premium. His sisters all lived in Denver, had made good marriages and borne children and even managed two careers between the three of them.

"My father died a few years ago," he said, "but my mom lives in Denver, to be close to my sisters and their children."

"I got the impression you were raised in the Springs."

He nodded, blotting his mouth with a paper napkin before speaking again. "She moved up there three or four years ago to be close to her grandbabies—of which she can never have enough." He grinned, eyes flashing with a wicked gleam. "If she met you, she'd have us married and making some more for her in a week."

Maggie never blushed, and she didn't now, but for once she saw a use for it. "You're terrible," she managed.

"I've had a lot of practice. I can still reduce my sisters to puddles of giggles in seconds." He trapped one of her ankles between both of his playfully. "I can also untie shoelaces with my toes," he teased, grinning. "Would you like to see?"

"I don't have shoelaces." She measured him over the table. "I feel sorry for your sisters."

He nodded cheerfully.

She munched on a French fry. Her ankle was firmly wedged between his, and it made her smile. Men tended to treat women as either something to conquer or something mysterious. Joel did neither. He was the kind of man who would take everything about a woman in stride, the kind of man who could debate birth control choices without batting an eye.

At this last example, she ducked her head, embarrassed at how often sensual thoughts assaulted her when she was in his presence.

As if he read her mind, he said suddenly, "Go out with me tonight."

The words opened a new vista in Maggie's mind, giving her a glimpse of a landscape she'd never seen. Then she remembered David. "I can't. My daughter's boyfriend is coming over for dinner."

He lifted her hand and brushed her palm with his fingertips. "Another night then."

"We'll see."

In spite of the fact that she pretended not to cook, Maggie did have one specialty—Mexican food. There was something, she thought late that afternoon, about the smell of the chilies and the color of the ingredients that made preparing it less odious than other foods.

Sam planned to bring David home with her after school. Maggie had rented several movies at Sam's request and had even, much to her own surprise, dusted and vacuumed the living room, finding pleasure in an ordinarily irritating job. She liked her home, she decided once again. The furniture was simple—contemporary couches and television and stereo mixed with an antique trunk, sewing machine table and radio. One wall of the living room held shelves filled with books and magazines, photographs and memorabilia.

When the house was finished and dinner was bubbling in the oven, she took out Mitchell's letter to read over a cup of coffee.

All her life, she'd had pen pals. Some were friends left behind when her father was transferred, some were people Maggie met via the huge network of dedicated letter writers she'd stumbled upon at the age of thirteen when she'd sent for a list of pen pals. Her letters had gone as far as England, Japan and Germany, and had served as a time of respite in an unhappy adolescence.

Of all the pen pals she'd ever had, Mitchell was the most unusual and the most entertaining. She rarely mentioned him to anyone because of the furor that arose, the cautions and worry the correspondence inevitably drew.

She understood the objections—if it hadn't been Galen who'd fostered the friendship, Maggie wouldn't have adopted a prison pen pal. In the beginning, she'd been leery of it anyway.

When Mitchell, in his first letter, had put forth the rules for their letters, her mind had been eased. No personal tidbits, he said. No photos, no descriptions, no backgrounds. They would discuss books and ideas, politics and religion. Period.

In seven years, he'd never broken the rule. What he needed, as Galen had insisted in the beginning, was a place to exercise his considerable intellect.

This letter was no different. He'd been analyzing the works of William Faulkner, and today the discussion centered around *Light in August*, one of Maggie's favorites. She'd read the book as a teenager, but as she read Mitchell's descriptions of scenes he'd particularly enjoyed, details of the novel flooded back into her mind. Funny, she thought, smiling as she refolded the sheaf of papers. They always seemed to be struck by the same details in books but never came up with the same interpretation of the material. She would have a lot to say about Faulkner in her next letter.

She checked on her enchiladas and started a salad just as Samantha and David came in, laughing and joking. "Hey, Mom," Sam called. "We're here."

As if she couldn't hear. Maggie smiled to herself. "I'm in the kitchen."

"Is there room for one more?" Sam asked, popping her head around the corner. Behind her, in the living room, Maggie heard a low voice mingling with David's tenor and even before Maggie saw the sparkle of mischief in Sam's deep green eyes, she knew who the mysterious extra guest would turn out to be.

She gave her daughter a suspicious glance. "You aren't matchmaking are you?" she asked quietly.

"No!" She came into the kitchen. "Mom, you should see how he eats," she whispered. "I don't think he knows how to cook at all."

Strike one, Joel Summer, Maggie thought with a wry grimace. The discovery of a flaw that actually counted against him gave her perverse pleasure, and she looked at her daughter. "There's more than enough for four. Ask him if he wants a beer."

Sam flashed a cheerful grin. "Great."

Joel came into the kitchen a little while later, carrying the beer Sam had taken to him. He leaned on the counter. "Are you sure you don't mind?" he asked.

"Positive. Sam said you don't eat very well." She grinned at him as she rolled up a concoction of flour tortillas, sliced black olives and sour cream. "I'm a good neighbor."

"Mmm," he murmured noncommittally. "Are you just being neighborly?" A playful skepticism underlined his words.

"You'd better behave or you'll have to go home," she said. "There are impressionable teenagers in the other room."

He laughed. "I'll be good," he said, but he moved close behind her, his voice a tangible caress. With one hand on her shoulder, near the edge of her blouse, he murmured, "How about if I go get some of my Jamaican coffee?"

Maggie had shifted, about to turn to agree, when she felt his firm lips press into the flesh of her shoulder. The contact sent a shudder all the way down her spine, into her legs. "Quit," she whispered, pushing him away. Concentrating on the task before her in order to avoid giving away her reaction, she said, "Go get your coffee."

Joel laughed and his hand lingered an instant longer. "Be right back."

"Dinner will be ready in a few minutes."

"Great," he said, smiling. "I'm starved."

As he left the kitchen, Maggie rolled her shoulders restlessly, trying to dislodge the tingling aftereffect of his lips on her skin.

It didn't work. She could still feel it as they sat down to dinner ten minutes later.

The four of them ate at the round kitchen table as the afternoon light deepened to a rich gold. There had been no rainstorm that day, and the air floating in through the back door was warm and scented heavily with lilacs.

Joel consumed the meal with genuine enthusiasm—Sam's estimation of his cooking abilities was an overstatement. He existed on frozen entrées and restaurant food. The blend of chilies, cheese and beef in Maggie's enchiladas was delicious. As he ate, he watched the woman who put them all at ease around her table.

Like the food, she had a southwestern flavor about her. A simple pale muslin blouse set off her tawny coloring, and a green print skirt flowed around long-muscled calves. Silver feather earrings dangled against her neck, and twisted ropes of silver circled her wrists. She laughed with the teens and told stories of her own, giving them her full attention when they talked.

That she was aware of him in return was evident to Joel in the way she avoided his eyes. Once, his feet and hers tangled under the table, and she shot an alarmed look his way. Otherwise, she studiously kept her eyes trained anywhere but upon him, even when he spoke. Her hands flitted nervously, she urged extra helpings on everyone and kept their glasses filled with ice cubes and tea. Inwardly, he smiled.

After dinner, Sam and Maggie cleaned up, and Maggie brewed the Jamaican coffee. Sam announced that she and David were going to take a walk. "Don't be gone too long," Maggie cautioned. She glanced toward Joel, standing in the sunlight pouring through the window. Nervousness rippled through her belly. "Do you want a cup of coffee, Joel?" she asked, folding the dish towel. "It's finished."

He looked over his shoulder at her, unmoving. The front screen door banged shut behind Samantha and David, and his chin lifted a little higher. It seemed to Maggie that he stood there against the light for an endless time, looking at her without a sound. She waited, watching his eyes grow brighter and clearer.

When he suddenly shifted toward her, she found herself wringing the dish towel through her fingers, unable to maintain the eye contact he hadn't broken as he moved across the room.

He stopped in front of her and took the towel out of her fingers. "You know I don't want a cup of coffee," he said. He wrapped his huge hands around her elbows. "But I do want you to stop looking like I'm going to eat you."

Maggie dipped her head briefly, smiling, then looked at him. "You make me so nervous."

"You're fighting your instincts," he murmured. He lifted her hands and placed them on his chest, then circled her waist with his arms. "Why's that?"

Maggie let her fingers spread on the flannel that covered his chest. She shook her head. "It's not that I don't know how," she protested and looked up. "It's just that—"

He cut her off with a kiss. And this, Maggie thought breathlessly, was no chaste exploration. With the same appetite he'd turned to his food, he tasted her lips; the edges and sides and tops; then the vulnerable inner flesh and the tip of her tongue. It was lazy and gluttonous at once, the craft of an expert.

Maggie melted, simply dissolved against him, feeling his sturdy thighs and hard belly against hers. She made a sound of pleasure, and Joel slid his hands over her waist and back, devouring her lips. Her arms looped up around his neck as she strained on tiptoe to reach him more completely. In her stomach, a pulse beat feverishly.

Joel released her mouth but secured her against him, leaning back to lift her clear off the floor. "God, I've wanted to do that all day," he said, and set her carefully down. His eyes swept her face and his hands ran up her sides, his thumbs grazing her breasts. Maggie moved against him instinctively, lifting her face to kiss him again.

This, she thought with a rush of passion, was what she had imagined when she'd heard his shower. It wasn't enough. She circled his husky, well-formed neck with her hands, unfurling her fingers to feel the heat of his skin on her palms. His coarse hair grazed her knuckles, prickly in contrast to the enticing and surprising velvet of his skin.

The very size of him excited Maggie, but it proved frustrating as well, for she couldn't reach him well enough to suit her—she wanted to touch the crown of his head and his shoulder blades; she wanted to strip them both bare and fall to the floor.

The animal nature of her thoughts startled her and effectively brought her back to earth. "Joel," she whispered, "Sam could walk in at any moment."

He kissed her quickly and lifted his head, smiling down. "You're right," he said, his voice a rumbling vibration Maggie felt through his chest. "And I promised to take it easy."

Maggie flashed a rueful smile of her own, touching his square jaw. "I'm a grown woman," she said. "I'm capable of saying no."

His eyes darkened to the color of the mountains on a hazy afternoon. "I'm having trouble saying no, myself. There's something about you—" He hugged her, then eased his hold.

"How about that coffee?" she asked. Somehow, she felt more relaxed than she had before. In spite of the weakness in her body, she felt richly confident and gracious.

He nodded reluctantly. "We can take it outside. I'd like to show you what I'm going to do with the garden."

Maggie, pouring coffee, bit her lip. "The garden?"

"You don't mind if I plant some vegetables, do you? It looks as fallow as the rest of the yard."

"Oh, no," she said hastily. "I don't mind at all." It was just that it made his occupancy of the apartment next door seem permanent. Until that moment, she hadn't really thought of him being next door every day, not just for the next month or so, but for the month after that and the one after that and the one after that.

Joel seemed to sense her misgivings in the way that he had of almost reading her mind—another point against him, she thought darkly. "Maggie," he said, brushing her cheek with his palm. "You don't have to be afraid of me."

"I just don't know anything about you, not really."

He grinned. "It takes a little time." The bantering mood fled abruptly as he stared at her, and she watched the ridge along his jaw go hard for an instant. "Trust your instincts, Maggie."

She swallowed. "I'll try."

The predawn darkness weighed like a live thing upon him, the silence an echo of other times, other places. Joel flung back the sheet and padded silently into the alcove off his bedroom. Here air blew through the windows, heavy with the scent of lilacs and night. He breathed in the freshness like an exhausted runner, and slowly, his panic attack began to calm. He stretched out on the pallet he had made in this room and turned on his tape player, letting the mellow guitar of Albert King soothe him.

He tried, as he lay there, to keep his despair at bay. Night sometimes brought the sorrows back to him, paraded before his insomniac eyes the life he had lost, the dreams that had been crushed, the long, dark years he couldn't always believe he'd escaped.

At times like this, he hated Nina with every molecule in his body, hated her for all she had stolen—his trust, his love, his life. As the emotion filled him with hard rage, red and black against his eyelids, he practiced again an exercise he'd learned. "God," he croaked into the night, "bless Nina. Bless Nina. Bless Nina." He repeated the phrase until the hate ebbed, losing its power over him.

His breathing returned to normal; his heartbeat slowed. The cool night air whispered over his face, like the gentle flutters of a butterfly wing. Just before sleep entirely carried him away, he thought of a smooth swath of honey-gold hair swinging around an angled face—and another emotion claimed him: guilt.

In the beginning, his plan had seemed so simple, a gamble he had no choice but to accept. Now he knew the gamble had been a selfish one.

He also knew he could not yet give it up.

Chapter Six

The next day Maggie arose early to fix Sam's favorite pecan waffles for breakfast. As she whipped up the batter, she saw Joel out in the garden, digging, but something about his still demeanor told her he thought himself to be unobserved, and she didn't call out to him through the open back door. Out of respect for his privacy—something she seemed to be forgetting he had a right to—she turned her attention fully to the waffles.

"Two decent meals in a row?" Samantha said in disbelief when she came downstairs. "Are you feeling okay?"

"This is my apology for judging a book by its cover."

Sam smiled. "Thank you."

"Sure."

As they ate, Sam said, "Mom?"

Maggie looked at her. "Samantha?"

"Do you think Dad would be upset if I didn't come stay with him this summer?"

Maggie cut a triangle of the golden brown waffle on her plate. "Does this have anything to do with David?"

"No—well, yes, but it's not because he asked me to ask." She poked a bubble of butter with her fork. "We're just getting along so well, I hate to see it end."

"What makes you think it will? You'll only be gone six weeks."

"Six weeks is a long time."

"I know it seems like it is, but it'll be gone before you know it." Maggie paused. "Your father would be devastated if you didn't come. He spends months freeing his schedule for your visits to Denver."

"I know, and I want to see him, too." Her voice dipped. "I'm just really going to miss David." Her clear eyes were troubled as they met Maggie's across the table. "It's kind of hard to choose."

"You can stay in touch—write letters, talk on the phone."

"What if he finds another girl while I'm gone? Somebody more like him?"

Maggie cut, lifted and chewed a bite of waffle while she mulled her reply. What she ought to say was "You'll find someone else," but she had a hunch that wasn't the answer Samantha sought. "I don't think you have to worry about that, Sam. He has more to worry about on that level than you do.''

Sam sighed deeply. ''It just seems like everybody is more hip than I am.''

''He had his choice of everybody, Sam. He chose you.''

Sam brightened. ''I never thought of it like that.''

Maggie raised her eyebrows, feeling very much like the sage advice columnist she became for the newspaper. ''Be yourself. It's all any of us really have.''

Sam nodded and ate in silence for a time. Suddenly, she asked, ''Did you love my dad?''

Maggie frowned. Where had that come from? ''I thought I did,'' she said with a sigh. ''He was so handsome and important and charming....'' She shook her head. ''He dazzled me, but it was you I loved.''

She'd been too young and inexperienced to see it then, but the truth of her words was plain in retrospect. Paul had been too busy for his little girl, a sunshine child of five with a demanding attitude that hid her need to be reassured and loved. Maggie thought she had been able to offset the insecurity Sam would have faced without a mother. A burst of pride and love consumed her as she studied her beautiful daughter. ''I wouldn't have traded it for the world.''

''Even though he ended up hurting you?''

''How do you know about that?''

''I'm not stupid. He's the same guy now as he was then.'' Sam rolled her eyes. ''I love my dad—don't get me wrong—but he's not good husband material.''

Maggie laughed.

Sam stretched lazily. "That was really good." She stood up and kissed Maggie on the forehead. As she carried her plate to the sink, she asked, "What about Joel?"

Maggie kept her eyes on her coffee cup, unwilling to take the chance that her feelings about him would show. "What about him?"

"He likes you, Mom," she said with an air of authority. "And I think he's pretty cute for an old guy."

"Don't matchmake me, Sam."

"I'm not," she protested. "But you aren't gonna be young forever, you know."

Maggie chuckled. "I'm delighted you think I have a few years left."

"I think you oughta go out with him again."

"I don't think it's any of your concern."

"Right." Sam tossed her head of bright hair. "Just trying to help." On her way out of the kitchen, she added, "But you also ought to wear that white dress. If he asks."

"I'll keep it in mind," Maggie said dryly. "Before we meet your great-grandmother for lunch, you need to check over your clothes to see if there's anything you need before you go to Denver."

"Dad always buys me new clothes."

"I mean panties and bras and socks. He never thinks of things like that." She squirted soap into hot water for the dishes. "We can get you some this afternoon—maybe even a pair of shoes."

"Not with Grandma—she'll examine every seam of every pair of underwear I like."

Maggie grinned. "You've obviously never shopped for lingerie with your great-grandmother."

"What do you mean?"

"You'll see. Go on, now. Get your shower so that we can leave—I don't want to wait an hour for you to do your hair."

"It's awfully early."

Maggie dumped the silverware into the water. "I'm not taking any chances. We have reservations at noon."

"I'm not that bad," Sam protested.

"Worse." A knock at the front door interrupted the conversation, and Sam dashed upstairs, afraid to be seen in her sweats. Maggie grinned to herself, wondering where her own sense of vanity had gone—she wasn't fit to greet the paperboy.

So, naturally, it was Joel at the door. "Hi," she said, brushing back a lock of hair.

"Are you busy? I could use a hand for a minute getting a curtain rod hung."

"A curtain rod?" she echoed blankly. "Oh—sure. Let me yell for Samantha and I'll be right out."

Sam appeared at the head of the stairs when Maggie called. "I'm going to run next door for a minute," Maggie said. "Hurry up and get in the shower."

Sam flashed a thumbs-up signal. "All right, Mom."

Maggie shook her head.

Joel waited on the porch, turning as he heard the screen creak open. Her feet were bare, her long legs exposed by the shorts, her hair free. Four bracelets adorned one wrist, expensive bracelets made with silver, agate, jade and what he thought might be lapis lazuli. In her ears were wide silver disks, their surface cratered like the moon. He grinned. "You're about half tomboy, half glamour girl, aren't you?"

Maggie gave him a twist of a smile. "You caught me in between modes."

He could see that she was a little embarrassed, and it pleased him. It meant his opinion mattered in some way. "Come on," he said, "in here."

As when he'd brought her in to meet the old tomcat, Maggie felt a little overwhelmed in his living room. This morning, she realized that one portion of the intimacy she felt was due to the scent of the room, a concentrated essence of the man himself, something rich and loamy and sun warmed.

"So, what do you need help with?"

"This," he said, and picked up one end of the sixty-inch drapery rod for the front picture window. "I've tried four times to get it hung, but it's impossible with one person. I need you to brace it in the middle while I nail the ends."

"I think I can handle that."

And it really should have been fairly simple, except the chair was just low enough to make it a stretch for Maggie to reach the center of the rod, and Joel had to return to the toolbox for different nails twice. Each time he whispered by her, she felt the aura of his body slam into her torso, a portion that seemed unnaturally exposed in her stretched position. Her awareness of him exaggerated a minute into a deep, still length of time, and she felt an absurd need to catch a bit more air into her lungs.

"You better hurry, Joel. I can't stand here like this all day."

He stood up. "What if I tickled you right now?" he said in his raspy voice.

"You wouldn't dare." The thought of his hands touching her exposed middle section set her nerves whirring from her eyelids to her shins. When a wisp of something curled around her ankle, she started, gave a strangled yelp—and tumbled right off the chair.

Joel snagged her, laughing, his powerful arms pulling her against his chest.

For one long, dazed second, she stared at the column of his throat, watching it move with the rumbling sound she could feel vibrating against her palms and into her belly.

He looked down at her. "It was only the cat. Are you okay?"

"Fine," she said, and made a move to release herself.

He tightened his arms. "I kind of like this," he said, one hand moving on her spine.

Fighting the impulse to dissolve against him as she had the night before, Maggie said breathlessly, "We're only supposed to see each other in broad daylight and in the company of lots of other people."

He released her gently. "Come on. Let's get this curtain rod up."

Oddly deflated, Maggie nodded and climbed back onto the chair. They finished the job without incident, and Maggie headed for the door.

Joel snagged her hand. "It was an excuse, you know—the curtain rod."

"Was it? For what?"

"To see you." His fingers sandwiched hers. The skin on his hands was dry and cool. "Go out with me tonight."

"Joel—" she began, her fear a palpable thing. If she continued to spend time with him, eventually her defenses would give way—they would become lovers.

He half grinned and the dimples flashed, making him look more like a teenager than a full-grown man. As always, it disarmed her. "You're still afraid of me," he said.

She drew her hand away from his and adopted her most sensible tone. "Joel, I'm not a woman that indulges in casual sex. I'm also not made of stone." She swallowed, forcing herself to look at him to say the next words. They weren't children, after all. "I can't be with you so much and not want to . . . well . . ." She paused.

"I know," he said, as if her confession was not a confession at all. He made a move to touch her, then crossed his arms over his chest. "I also understand and respect your wishes. We'll go get some supper—maybe Guiseppe's or something." He reached to brush a finger over her arm. "I won't even hold your hand," he said with a smile. "Promise. Cross my heart and hope to die."

Maggie laughed. "You wretch. You know I want to say yes."

"What time?"

"I'll be ready about six-thirty," she said, moving toward the door. "And I have to be in by ten-thirty."

Joel nodded, trying to push the fullness from his chest, a fullness of anticipation that made him feel younger than he had ever felt, more alive than he had ever thought he'd be. "I'll be there."

Although Maggie tried to keep her mind on the moment at hand throughout the afternoon she spent with Samantha and her grandmother, she knew she was distracted. She barely tasted lunch, her mind was so focused on the upcoming dinner. She listened with a vague smile to the conversation between Anna and Samantha as they all lazily window-shopped, her mind floating toward Joel, wherever he was.

Her preoccupation didn't go unnoticed. "You look like the cat that ate the canary," Anna said, tapping Maggie on the arm.

"She went over to Joel's house this morning," Sam added teasingly. "When she came back, her face was full of color."

Maggie thanked the stars that she didn't blush, and ducked her head to hide her expression. Denying Sam's statement would only lead to more teasing, more protestations—so she kept quiet.

"Must be something," Anna said to Sam. "She always clams up when it's something big."

Maggie felt a grin stretch her mouth. "Come on, you guys," she pleaded. "Don't do this."

"Don't you trust us?" Sam teased.

"I trust you," she said, and shrugged. "I just feel silly."

"I'd feel silly over a man like that myself," Anna said.

Maggie laughed. "Okay, okay. I'm going out to dinner with him tonight. It's no big deal." She ignored the exchange of triumphant glances between Anna and Sam, pointing to the display of dolls in a toy store window. "Look at Rapunzel."

"Do you remember when we used to come here when you were a little girl?" Anna said.

"Of course."

"You never let me out of going there. We spent hours looking at those dolls." She frowned quizzically. "Didn't you finally get one?"

"Yes, don't you remember? Galen saved for a year when he was fourteen to buy me Beth from *Little Women* for Christmas."

"Uncle Galen did that?" Sam asked. "Gee, I don't think I could save money for that long."

"He's not like anyone else in the world," Maggie said fondly. She touched her grandmother's arm. "He's going to come here for his vacation this summer—I don't think I told you."

Samantha stopped in her tracks. "When?"

"I'm not sure. But if you're still in Denver, we might be able to work it out for you to come down for a few days. I'm sure your father won't object."

Anna sniffed audibly. Maggie smiled to herself.

"You notice how she changed the subject?" Sam said, winking.

"Let's go find some underclothes for you," Maggie said, resolutely ignoring the comment.

"My favorite part," Anna said.

"Just remember, Gram. This isn't Paris."

Anna waved her hand in dismissal. "A woman with beautiful underwear is a beautiful woman."

It was a sentiment Maggie tried to remember later as she slipped into the fragile chemise her grandmother had pushed into her hands at the last minute. She didn't feel very beautiful as she tried to decide what to do with her hair, which blouse to wear, which earrings.

She was ready too early. Her palms were sweaty, her heart unsteady. With an edge of hysteria, Maggie thought, I'm as nervous as a twelve-year-old!

She tried to trick herself into a state of calm by watering the handful of neglected plants that struggled to survive in various corners around the house. She wiped the counters in the kitchen, straightened the magazines on the coffee table, plumped the pillows on the couch.

When the doorbell rang, she was perched uneasily on the edge of a kitchen chair, staring at the newspaper. The bell sent an additional—and definitely unnecessary—surge of adrenaline through her veins, making her hands tremble so violently she could barely open the door.

The lunacy of her reaction struck her as she opened the door to Joel. He wore a crisp, pale gray shirt with slender rose and blue stripes, open at the neck, and his freshly washed hair still showed shower dampness. His dark cheeks were newly shaved, and he smelled like soap and cologne.

Although she felt the familiar leap in her pulse at the pleasure of looking at him, she also realized he was much more than handsome. He was a man she'd grown to like very much the past few weeks, a man whose company made her feel warm and comfortable in spite of the leaping sexual awareness he aroused. The knowledge calmed her as nothing else could have.

"Hi," she said. "You look great."

He grinned. "Thanks. So do you."

"Let me grab a jacket and I'll be ready to go." She took a jacket from the coatrack near the door and folded it over her arm.

"No purse?"

"I know it's ridiculous, but I never got the knack of carrying one," she said, stepping out onto the porch. "I buy clothes with pockets, instead."

"Seems to work for me."

"I'm glad to hear it," Maggie said as she walked with him to his truck. "You'd look silly with a purse."

He half grinned, a habitual gesture of irony. "Bet no one would question my right to carry it."

She laughed. "Probably not."

Guiseppe's, an Italian restaurant in a transformed train depot, was crowded. As they waited in the foyer for a table, Maggie said, "This is beautiful. I've never been here—at least since it's been a restaurant."

"I think you'll like it." With a twinkle in his eye, he added, "I knew I'd have to pick someplace where they really feed you."

"Are you implying that I'm a big eater?"

He squeezed her hand playfully. "Honey, I've seen you eat."

Maggie raised her eyebrows with a smile. In a mirror along the wall, she caught sight of a well-tended young woman eyeing Joel surreptitiously, her gaze sweeping over him with deep appreciation. Almost as if the woman felt Maggie noticing, she glanced up and caught Maggie's eyes in the mirror. With an apologetic smile, she shrugged as if to say, I couldn't help myself. Maggie grinned and tried to remember what the conversation had been about before she'd been distracted. "I'm probably going to be fat as Santa Claus by the time I'm fifty."

"I don't think so." Lazily and boldly, he let his gaze wander over her body, and Maggie felt an answering tingle follow behind each spot as his eyes passed it. She shifted.

"Our table is ready," she said, thankful for the distraction.

The hostess led them through a narrow aisle to a booth in the back. The sounds of dozens of diners, racy music on the speakers, the chatter of the busboys and the waitresses calling out their orders gave the air a charged excitement. Maggie breathed in the atmosphere, smelling garlic and tomatoes and brewing coffee. Their booth was nestled in a stone cove, a private and intriguing spot.

After examining every item, Maggie finally took Joel's advice and ordered the lasagna. As they settled back to wait for the meal, Maggie asked, "Are you really a bad cook?"

Joel laughed. "Worse than bad. I don't know how."

"Why don't you learn?"

"Oh, I am, slowly. The microwave helps."

"What I don't understand is why it's taken you so long," Maggie said with a hint of reproval. "No woman would play helpless like that."

He shrugged good-naturedly. "I've always had someone to cook for me."

"How did you manage that?"

It seemed an innocent enough question, but Maggie sensed his walls coming up in defense, saw them in the odd set of his shoulders and jaw. He shrugged.

"You have a lot of secrets, Joel Summer," she said. "One day I hope you can share some of them."

He swallowed and looked at her. "I hope so, too."

She let the mystery drift away. For now it was enough to laugh at the stories they told each other. Maggie heard herself making humorous things that had been terribly painful at the time they happened, laughing ruefully at the overly serious and sensitive child she had been. She even managed to caricature her father to the point that she could laugh just a little, even about him.

Joel listened and laughed and offered tidbits of his own life: the way he had manipulated dinner conversations to start arguments between his sisters, the panic he once had when he wrecked his parents' car at the age of seventeen, the practical jokes he'd played on teachers.

When the food came, Maggie salted and peppered her dish, then added a generous helping of grated Romano cheese. She glanced up to find Joel watching her. "Did I miss something?"

"I bet you like chili dogs with onions and cheese, too, don't you?"

Maggie grinned. "And anything else sloppy and greasy and full of preservatives. Samantha is always after me to alter my diet to include some fresh vegetables."

"Don't you get heartburn?"

"Not yet." She looked at him. "You don't like sloppy food?"

He shook his head. "I was one of those kids who divided his plate into sections. I ate all the peas, then all the roast, then the carrots—like that."

"Did you have a system, or did you just start with whatever looked good at the time?"

"Color coded. Lightest to darkest."

Maggie swallowed. "Really?"

He concentrated for a moment on cutting his food, then swept his glittering blue eyes open to meet hers. "No." He smiled.

"Oh, you." Maggie tsked and bit into her lasagna. "You were the kind of boy I wanted to drown in a water fountain when I was in junior high."

"Probably. And I would have put frogs in your locker because I knew it."

After their dinner, Joel said, "I've got dessert in the truck."

"In the truck?"

He grinned, picking up the check. "Don't give me that suspicious look—I promised, didn't I?" He stood up and held out a hand. "I have a surprise for you."

She hesitated a moment more, then shook her head with a smile and let him help her up. As she followed him out, she thought she liked the boyishness of his personality. He was mature, even serious where it concerned matters of the world and his career, but the unquenchable boy within allowed him to wring every drop of pleasure from a good moment.

He drove to a hilly park located in the middle of one of the most frantic areas of the city. As he drove past houses built at the edges of the wooded park, heading for the summit of a hill, he remarked, "When I was a kid, there was nothing out here at all."

"I never came out this far. My grandmother's always lived on the west side."

"I'm told," he said with a wicked smile, "that a great many children were conceived under the shelter of these trees."

Maggie raised her eyebrows and refused to acknowledge the gambit.

"Did you ever park in high school?" he asked.

"I'm not telling," she said with a laugh. "Did you?"

"I'd lie and say I did, even if I hadn't, wouldn't I?"

"I guess men do have an image to uphold."

"Better believe it."

He turned the truck into a level parking area that overlooked the expanding eastern edge of the city. "Do you want a beer?" he asked, turning off the engine.

"Sure."

"Let's sit outside. It's beautiful tonight."

He fished two bottles of beer out of a cooler in the back of the truck and spread a blanket on the ground for them to sit on.

"What about dessert?" Maggie asked, teasing.

"Oh." He held up one finger and scrambled in the glove compartment, bringing out two Hershey's bars.

"Beer and chocolate?"

"Don't knock it till you try it." He handed her one of the candy bars, then settled down next to her on the blanket, cross-legged and comfortable.

"Did you come here with your wife?" Maggie asked. As soon as the words left her lips, she wanted to call them back.

But Joel didn't seem to mind. "Only with her. We met in ninth grade." He held up his bottle to the shimmering glow of red and green and white lights from below, seeming to measure them through the golden beer. "How about you?"

"I was too afraid of my father to do any of that. If I had shown up with a hickey on my neck or something, he would have killed me."

"A hard core." Joel nodded. "Where is he now?"

Silhouette's

Best Ever "Get Acquainted" Offer

Look what we'd give to hear from you

Look what we've got for you:

5 FREE GIFTS

... A FREE 20k gold electroplate chain
... plus a sampler set of 4 terrific Silhouette Special Edition® novels, specially selected by our editors.

FREE MYSTERY GIFT

... PLUS a surprise mystery gift that will delight you.

All this just for trying our Reader Service!

If you wish to continue in the Reader Service, you'll get 6 new Silhouette Special Edition® novels every month—before they're available in stores. That's SNEAK PREVIEWS for just $2.74* per book—21¢ less than the cover price—and FREE home delivery besides!

Plus There's More!

With your monthly book shipments, you'll also get our newsletter, packed with news of your favorite authors and upcoming books—FREE! And as a valued reader, we'll be sending you additional free gifts from time to time—as a token of our appreciation for being a home subscriber.

THERE IS NO CATCH. You're not required to buy a single book, ever. You may cancel Reader Service privileges anytime, if you want. All you have to do is write "cancel" on your statement or simply return your shipment of books to us at our cost. The free gifts are yours anyway. It's a super-sweet deal if ever there was one. Try us and see!

Get 4 FREE full-length Silhouette Special Edition® novels.

Plus

this lovely 20k gold
electroplate chain

Plus

a surprise
free gift

▼ **PLUS LOTS MORE! MAIL THIS CARD TODAY** ▼

Silhouette's Best-Ever "Get Acquainted" Offer

Yes, I'll try Silhouette books under the terms outlined on the opposite page. Send me 4 free Silhouette Special Edition® novels, a free electroplated gold chain and a free mystery gift.

235 CIS RIYK (U-S-SE-03/90)

```
PLACE STICKER
FOR 6 FREE GIFTS
HERE
```

NAME _____

ADDRESS _____ APT. _____

CITY _____

STATE _____ ZIP CODE _____

Offer limited to one per household and not valid to current Silhouette Special Edition Subscribers. All orders subject to approval. Terms and prices subject to change without notice. © 1989 HARLEQUIN ENTERPRISES LTD.

PRINTED IN U.S.A.

Don't forget...

... Return this card today and receive 4 free books, free electroplated gold chain and free mystery gift.

... You will receive books before they're available in stores.

... No obligation to buy. You can cancel at any time by writing "cancel" on your statement or returning a shipment to us at our cost.

If offer card is missing, write to: Silhouette Books®
901 Fuhrmann Blvd., P.O. Box 1867, Buffalo, N.Y. 14269-1867

BUSINESS REPLY CARD
First Class   Permit No. 717   Buffalo, NY

Postage will be paid by addressee

Silhouette® Books
901 Fuhrmann Blvd.
P.O. Box 1867
Buffalo, NY 14240-9952

No Postage
Necessary
If Mailed
In The
United States

Maggie lifted one shoulder. "I have no idea. My mother divorced him when I was seventeen, and we never heard a word from him again."

"I'm sorry, Maggie."

"Don't be." She lifted her head. "All he ever did was make us miserable, anyway." She looked at him, at the disbelief in his eyes. "Really."

He looked at her for a long moment. "You need to forgive him, Maggie."

"For what? I think he did the best he could," she said lightly. But in contrast to her words, in her memory her father hacked away hunks of her brother's hair as Galen screamed. She looked at Joel. "I really don't like to talk about my father."

"Okay," he answered easily.

"How are your birds?" Maggie asked, lifting her beer.

"We got a bald eagle today—gunshot in the wing."

"A bald eagle? Isn't that against the law?"

Wryly, he said, "So is burglary."

"I know, but although I don't approve of burglary, I can understand the profit motive behind it. Why would anyone shoot an eagle?"

"The feathers alone will bring in a fortune, not to mention the trophies of heads and feet." He sighed. "People are responsible for almost all the injuries we see. The birds get stuck in traps, are poisoned by pesticides or shot."

"All because of the feathers?" Maggie asked incredulously.

"No, not at all. That's mainly eagle feathers—the hawks and falcons and vultures are shot because people don't really understand them. Farmers think hawks will carry off their baby animals." He used his hands to draw on the air. "Most of the other kinds of problems are accidental."

"Will they carry off babies?" She thought she could understand a shooting based on protecting baby animals.

"Maybe, once in a while. But killing the birds isn't the answer. It's like killing coyotes because they steal a few chickens—pretty soon you're overrun with rodents of all kinds."

"The big birds keep the rodents under control?"

"Are you just humoring me, or do you really find this interesting?"

"I'm playing with the idea of doing a feature on your career for the end-of-summer issue," Maggie said with a grin. "It's exactly the kind of profession I like to highlight. Intriguing, different, something most teens wouldn't have heard anything about."

"That's great. I'd love to see you do it."

"You're a good candidate because you so obviously love what you're doing."

He smiled. "Thanks."

"Now, finish with the rodents."

Joel shifted, sipped his beer. "One pair of mice can spawn a million descendants in a year."

"A million?" she echoed.

"A million. One red-tailed hawk eats about fifteen hundred to two thousand mice a year."

"Wow."

Joel touched her arm and pointed to the horizon. "Get ready."

A pause fell between them. He gestured with one strong arm for Maggie to move into the hollow he made for her. She sat in front of him, her head nestled in his shoulder, her back against his chest. His legs rested easily along the outside of hers.

From the edge of the eastern horizon, there came a great light, an orb of orange lifting like a newly created planet to grace the night sky. Without realizing it, Maggie leaned forward, entranced by the sight of the full moon rising, so huge and bright, from the darkness. She sighed, pressing a hand to her chest.

"It's really something, isn't it?" Joel murmured, his hands in her hair.

She nodded very slowly, her heart filling with a soft illumination, as gentle as the man now cradling her. She shifted to look at him. His face was bathed with the light, his eyes almost mystical as they reflected the great, round moon. "Thank you," she breathed.

There was no resisting him as he bent his head to fit his mouth to hers. There was no demand in his tender and playful exploration of her lips. His tongue snaked out to hers, and his hands combed gently through her hair.

It was a deceptive ease and care he took, an effort to remain calm that made his hands tremble. Maggie sensed his restraint with a feeling of frustration, and she turned in his embrace, pulling away from his sweet kiss. She nuzzled his neck, smelling the clean after-shave he wore, working her hand up his shirt to its opening. She slipped her fingers beneath the flannel to his chest and kissed his neck with her tongue. When his grip tightened reflexively around her, she smiled.

"Isn't this the kind of thing you do when you park? Neck?"

He laughed low in his chest.

For a while, Maggie thought he wasn't going to say anything, and when he did, it was in a voice so deep that it was nearly a growl.

"Every situation demands a different response."

With disappointment, and relief, Maggie realized he would stick to his promise—even if in her heart, she didn't want him to.

"We ought to get back," he said, standing up.

Maggie sighed. "I suppose you're right." She fell back on the blanket, staring up to the sky. "Too bad."

"Are you a camper?" Joel asked.

"I don't know. I've never tried it." She felt a tickle on her neck and brushed it absently. "Are you?"

He affected a country drawl. "Since I was knee-high to a grasshopper."

Maggie nodded distractedly. The tickle moved higher on her neck, and she reached for it again. When her fingers encountered the unmistakable shape of a spider, she shrieked and jumped to her feet, batting madly at her neck.

"What is it?" Joel asked in alarm.

A shudder passed through her. "A spider." She brushed her neck and shook her hair hard. Another shudder rippled her shoulders. "Ugh!"

Joel laughed. "I wouldn't have put frogs in your locker if I'd ever seen you act like that over a spider."

Maggie strove to see the humor in the situation but revulsion clouded everything. "Joel, please see if he's on my back or anywhere."

He bit his lip to contain the grin, but he did as he was asked. "All clear." With an obvious effort to maintain a straight face, he asked, "Are you all right now?"

"Fine," she said, her voice thick with the disgust she felt toward herself. Briskly, she bent over to yank up the blanket, then shook it viciously. "Believe it or not, I used to pay my brother to kill spiders for me."

"Poor Maggie," he said, but laughter lingered in his voice.

Resolutely, she ignored him. "I feel sorry for your sisters," she said haughtily.

He choked and finally burst out laughing. "I'm sorry," he said when he caught the look of dignified endurance on her face. He swallowed the last chuckles, but his nostrils quivered for a moment longer as she carefully folded the blanket.

"You know," he said, "I've read that a fear of spiders is related to low endorphins in your brain. You know how we could increase your endorphins, don't you?"

Maggie gave him a dry glance. "Don't even say it, Joel Summer. It's bad enough you're a tease. You don't have to prove yourself to be a lecher, as well."

He shrugged. "Just trying to be helpful."

* * *

Moses, Joel's cat, was waiting on the front porch when they got back. With him was a kitten, perhaps four or five months old. It was a scrawny gray tiger, with tufts of white at its chest and paws. As Joel and Maggie came up the walk, Moses shifted, like a child getting ready to ask a favor, and protectively licked the kitten's ear.

"Who's this, Moses?" Joel asked, squatting. He held his fingers out to the kitten, who sniffed them delicately and rubbed against the other cat. Moses meowed softly.

Maggie had never seen a cat behave in such a territorial fashion toward an animal it hadn't lived with. As she watched, the kitten stood up and haltingly limped toward Joel. "Oh, he's hurt," Maggie said.

Joel scooped him up, his hands easily engulfing the skinny body. Moses meowed again and trotted to the front door. Joel grinned. "Okay. I get the message. We'll take him inside." He looked at Maggie, a bemused smile on his face. "Have you ever seen such a thing?"

Maggie shook her head, following Joel inside at his indication. He carried the kitten into the kitchen and flipped on the overhead light.

The gray tiger was exhausted and trusting as Joel moved his fingers gently over its body. "Ah, I see," he murmured out loud. To Maggie, trying to calm Moses as he paced around, he said, "It looks like he might have got caught under the wheel of a car. His back paw is pretty mangled."

"Poor thing."

Joel squatted and Moses hurried over to wash the kitten with a few short whips of his tongue. "We'll take care of him, Moses," he said, reaching out to stroke the old tom gently. "Now, I bet you're hungry." He looked again at Maggie. "There's a bag of food in that cupboard. Would you feed him while I find a box to transport the kitten to the vet?"

"Of course." She moved to the cabinet, and Moses followed her eagerly. As she shook food into his dish, she marveled at the transformation of the mangy, distrustful animal into this glossy-coated, clean and loving cat. She rubbed his back fondly as he ate. "You found a master worth your time, didn't you?"

Joel had disappeared onto the back porch, and she heard him rustling around in there. "Do you need some help?" she asked, going to investigate.

A clatter greeted her, and as Maggie peeked into the glassed-in room he used as a recycling area, she grinned. "Having trouble?"

He sighed ruefully, the kitten clasped gently to his chest as he rooted around in a fifty-five gallon drum. "I thought I had a box that would work in here. I must have been wrong."

In the yellow light cast by the bulb overhead, his utterly straight hair shone as if polished, slightly mussed by the long evening. A photograph of him in his flannel shirt, so huge and muscled and rugged, with the tiny kitten clasped to his chest, would sell a million bottles of whatever anyone wanted to sell. She shifted.

Joel moved out of the corner. "I was going to invite you upstairs to see my etchings, but I've got to get this kitten to a vet."

"You've clearly been cast as hero," she agreed with a smile. "I understand."

He walked her to the door. Still holding the kitten, he bent to kiss her, touching her cheek gently. "I know the first part of the week is a busy time for you, but maybe we can get together Thursday or Friday."

"I'd like that." She reached up to brush the gloss of his hair with her fingers. Meeting his eyes, she said, "I had a wonderful time tonight."

He kissed her again, lingering this time. "So did I."

"Let me know how the kitten is."

"I will."

There was nothing else to do. Maggie walked out his door to her own. Immediately, the world seemed silent and a little lonely.

Chapter Seven

Mom, have you seen my red dress?"

Maggie smiled to herself. "I'm ironing it right now."

A sheepish Sam rounded the corner of the kitchen, where Maggie stood over the built-in ironing board. A basket of wrinkled clothing awaited her ministrations with the iron.

"I do this every year, don't I?" Sam commented. "Wait until the last minute to get things together and then spend days running around like a chicken with my head cut off."

"No, you're doing much better than usual this year. It's only Tuesday evening. Your father won't be here till a week from Saturday." Of course, Maggie thought, this year Samantha had motivation. Next Friday was the last day of school, and Sam planned to spend the afternoon and evening with David.

"Has Uncle Galen said anything more about when he's going to come?"

"You know how he is, Sam. He'll be here when he gets here." She eased the pointed nose of the iron into a nook under the collar of the red dress. "Don't worry. You'll only be seventy miles away. I'm sure we can work something out."

"Can Dad come down with me?"

"If he wants to." Maggie smiled. "Don't worry about me."

Sam gathered up a pile of clean clothes from the dryer, located in a closet in the kitchen, glanced once more at her mother and went back upstairs.

Maggie hung the dress on a hanger and shook a blouse from the mound of clothes at her feet. Since Samantha had begun to date David, she had been very concerned about the broken heart she assumed Maggie had suffered at the hands of her father. Nothing Maggie said would convince the girl that she had long ago recovered from any jilting. Deep in the throes of her first love, Sam couldn't conceive of loving anyone else again.

Fondly, she sighed. As always, the closer the time for Samantha to go to Denver came, the bluer Maggie got. She missed Sam on the long, hot days of June and July, missed her energy and quick spurts of excitement. She missed having three curling irons tangling in the bathroom drawer, MTV blaring and the burbling of conversations as Sam talked on the phone.

Get used to it, Maggie, she told herself. In two years, Samantha would graduate from high school and go on to her own life in college or in New York, whichever she chose when the time came. After that, Samantha would never really be hers again.

Maggie had never considered having a baby in spite of her own youth because Sam had filled that portion of her life so well and completely. Now, every so often she wondered what it would be like to experience pregnancy and birth and the tender helplessness of an infant.

The phone rang. Maggie started to cross the room to answer it, but hearing Sam's running footsteps in the hall overhead, decided not to join the race. She never got phone calls anymore, anyway.

To her surprise, Samantha called her. "Sharon's on the phone."

A clutch of uneasiness rippled through her belly. "Hi, Sharon," she said into the phone.

"You know it's a story at this time of night. Three guesses which one."

"Damn." Maggie sighed. Tickets for Proud Fox were going on sale at seven tomorrow morning, and even at five this afternoon, there had been a handful of kids armed with sleeping bags and cans of soda and sandwiches outside the ticket outlet. Everyone wanted good seats for the show. "I'll meet you in ten minutes."

She hung up the phone and switched off the iron. "Sam!" she called upstairs as she slipped into a pair of white leather tennis shoes. When her daughter appeared on the stairs, she said, "I have to go out for a while. Remember you have a final tomorrow."

"Is it the Proud Fox thing?"

"Yes." She frowned. "Is David there?"

"No, he had to work tonight."

Maggie nodded, heading for the door. "I don't know how long I'll be. Call your great-grandmother if you get lonely."

"Can I go with you?" Sam bit her lip. "Please?"

After a ten-second hesitation, Maggie acquiesced. "All right. Hurry."

She was rewarded with a dazzling grin from Samantha. "I just want to get my camera." She dashed up the stairs. Maggie donned a light woolen jacket with voluminous pockets, checking to be certain she had her pen and reporter's notebooks.

When Sam dashed down the stairs, her camera had been slung around her neck, and her hair was pulled severely into a ponytail. She'd thrown a sweatshirt over her jeans. In her green eyes was leaping excitement.

"Ready," she said breathlessly.

At the ticket outlet, Maggie couldn't believe the cacophony that slammed into her ears. From a dozen boom-boxes turned full volume blasted several different songs, all written by Proud Fox. Long-haired teenagers sang along to whatever song was closest to them. A few danced in the square fronting the department store where the tickets would go on sale the next morning.

In contrast, at the opposite end of the square, a large group of protesters marched solemnly in a circle, singing a hymn of long-suffering.

Maggie shook her head. Only teenagers could create this much melodrama—the costumes so extreme and opposed, the gravity of one group played against the hedonism of the other.

She turned to Samantha as they entered the square, looking for Sharon. "Don't get in the middle of anything," she said to Samantha. "And don't be too obvious with the camera. People will do anything to get their picture taken."

Sam nodded. She nervously licked her bottom lip and lifted the camera to ready f-stops and light settings. "Do you think I have enough light to shoot without a flash?"

"I don't know." The square was patchily lighted with overhead spots. "Try it and see what happens. I'm going to go talk to the protesters."

Sam nodded, shooting a wide-angle view of the scene, already engrossed in her photography. Maggie smiled as she watched Sam glance over the camera to measure the scene, then duck back behind it, never missing a step.

Maggie headed for the circle of protesters. When no one even glanced her way, she chose one young man at random and fell in step beside him. "I'm Maggie Henderson," she said. "I'd like to do a feature article, in depth, on what you're trying to do here."

The boy licked his lips. "The signs speak for themselves."

"Not really," she insisted. "There are dozens of bands with violent or sexual lyrics. Why are you opposed to Proud Fox in particular?"

He glanced at her and Maggie sensed he was nervous. "You need to talk to Cory."

"Okay," she agreed. "Point him out to me."

"He's, uh, not here right now. He said he'd join us later."

"Do you know where I can find him?"

"No." The answer was abrupt, and he glanced over his shoulder toward some of the other teens, who threw them sharply censorious looks.

"A last name?"

"I said he'll be here later. You can talk to him then."

The straggled line of campers waiting for tickets was growing louder and rowdier. From the corner of her eye, Maggie saw the uniformed police officer edging closer to the line, and she took a breath. She'd had no luck with the protesters. Maybe she could appeal to the rockers.

She reached the head of the line. "Hey!" she shouted to the girl who had the enviable position of being first in line.

The girl, no more than seventeen, turned her boombox down and looked at Maggie expectantly.

"You'd hate to lose this spot." Maggie said, still yelling. "If you can't help me get everybody quieted, the police will make you all go home."

The girl hesitated, then turned to talk to the boy right behind her. He measured Maggie for a minute and turned to the boy behind him, who nodded and turned his box down.

Maggie repeated the ploy about halfway through the line. The simple fact that they might lose their chance to buy tickets for the concert of the summer was more than enough inducement. With a sigh of satisfaction, she noted the sound levels lowering considerably, enough that the chanting hymn could be heard.

The shouts that signaled the onset of the riot were like a backfiring muffler on a quiet side street. Maggie turned in shock to see bodies from both sides, exploding into sudden violence.

At the sight of roiling bodies and police and flashing lights, her heart constricted. She'd glimpsed Sam a few seconds before the ruckus had broken out. Maggie prayed she'd had the sense to maintain her distance.

But she hadn't. Maggie glimpsed the tall, slender girl skirting the very edges of the action, shooting pictures as fast as she could click the shutter. Her cheeks were stained with a flush of high delight, her forehead dewed with sweat. And, Maggie noted as she neared her, Samantha's feet were bare.

For a long, long second, she simply watched as Samantha dipped and knelt and squatted and stretched to catch the best photos, her blond ponytail dancing as if to emphasize her exuberance. There was no high in the world, Maggie thought, like doing what you loved.

A crash of something behind her shook Maggie out of her reverie, and she made a lunge for Sam, catching her shirt to drag her away just as several more bodies hurtled by. They searched the crowd for Sharon, finding her with a boy who bore a long cut on his mouth. He struggled to shake free of Sharon, mumbling, "I'll be all right, I tell ya."

"Your arm is broken," the photographer argued with the deceptive sweetness she sometimes adopted to make a point. "No concert in the world is worth going through the rest of your life a cripple."

For the next hour, as police managed to calm the crowd and shoo away any lingering trouble, paramedics attended the wounded. Anyone who hadn't been hurt while waiting in line was told to go home, and the police had to haul off two more kids in squad cars when they resisted the orders.

By the time the last teens had been loaded into ambulances or police cars or sent home, Maggie was exhausted. "Sam," she said, "give your film to Sharon. She'll develop it."

"I might have gotten some good stuff," Sam said, handing over the roll.

Sharon gave her a playful punch. "You're a pro, kid. You kept your head and your eye. I'd bet my next paycheck that you've got a shot or two in here worth the morning paper."

Sam squealed, grabbing Sharon's hands. "Really?"

"Really."

Maggie grinned. "Do you have any idea where you might have left your shoes?"

"Uh—no." Sam glanced at the mess in the square and widened her eyes sheepishly. "I think they might be lost."

"It's all right." Maggie slung an arm around her daughter's shoulders. "But, in the future, you might think about wearing more comfortable shoes."

Sam smiled.

"Now, I've got an editorial to write while I'm still hot, and you have a final to study for."

"If you're going to be up awhile, Maggie, I'll call to let you know what we have in the way of photos," Sharon said.

"Great. Talk to you then."

Samantha barely spoke on the way home, deep in her own reverie. Maggie let her drift within herself, familiar with the need to absorb what had just been recorded. As they drove up in front of the house, Sam reached out to touch Maggie's hand. "Thanks for letting me go," she said.

Maggie smiled, touched again with the bittersweet evidence of Sam's growing maturity. "You're more than welcome."

She didn't see Joel until they reached the stairs. "Hi," he said, standing to greet them. In his arms was the kitten, his back paw rather conspicuously bandaged in a cast.

"Hi, Joel," Sam said cheerfully. "How's the kitten?"

"Good. The vet said today his lungs are clearing, and he should be able to eat real food in a few more days."

"He's so cute," Sam cooed, stepping forward to rub the kitten's head. "I'm glad he's okay." She tsked lightly. "I have to go study. See you guys later."

Maggie had watched the exchange with an amused smile. When Samantha went inside, she said, "I didn't know you and Samantha had grown to be friends."

"She comes to talk to me in the garden sometimes." He grinned. "She's the one who told me how much you love a certain brand of hamburger."

"Of course." Maggie grinned. "Count yourself among the elite, then. She finds most people over the age of twenty boring beyond belief."

"She's a sweet kid," he said. "But not nearly as sweet as her mother."

Maggie stared at him in the lamplighted dimness. His expression was tender and grave. A square of light caught on the plane of his cheekbone, throwing his eye into shadow. "I have to go in," she said, suddenly overwhelmed with the emotions crowding into her chest.

He moved slowly toward her and put a hand on her neck. "Do you have to go right now?"

"I have to write an editorial tonight, while I'm still angry."

"Well, then," he murmured, "go write and come back."

He pulled her head to his, his huge hand cupping the back of her skull, and lowered his mouth. Instead of kissing her gently, he took her lower lip into his mouth and sucked lightly. Her hips went weak with the sensation.

His thumb moved on her ear, stroking lightly, his touch jingling her earring, and he followed the sucking motion with a gentle nip and a teasing thrust of his tongue. "Come back out when you're done," he whispered insistently. "We can have some coffee or something."

"It might be a while."

"I can wait." His thumb moved up and down, up and down on her throat. "It's a beautiful night."

Maggie nodded. "Okay."

He let his hand slide down her arm, then squeezed her fingers and let go. "Go get finished. I'll be here."

But the editorial Maggie had planned to write completely disappeared from her mind when she sat down to try to scribble it out at the desk in her bedroom. She found herself glancing out to the backyard, her mind filled with the promise of Joel. In exasperation, she threw down her pencil.

Lately, her discipline had flown right out the window. Several times recently, when she should have been taking notes for a story or an editorial, she'd instead played peacemaker. Tonight, she'd been more interested in Sam's excitement than in the news unfolding around her. Even now, instead of writing an editorial, she wanted to find out who the students involved in the protest were and have a talk with the adults behind them. She wanted to stage a town meeting to call parents' attention to Proud Fox's lyrics. She wanted to find out why David could come and go at will, with no one paying much notice; she wanted to uncover the reasons why so many sixteen and seventeen-year-olds had been able to camp out all night in front of that store.

She had no interest in making a story out of it. She wanted to fix it.

Rubbing her forehead wearily, she let go of a long breath. Newspapers had once seemed to be the most exciting kind of career she could choose. After seeing Samantha at work shooting photographs tonight, Maggie realized there was a huge gap between what she felt for her career and what people who loved theirs felt. Like Joel. His voice soared when he spoke of hawks, and his eyes took on a glow.

It called into question everything she thought she knew about herself.

"Oh, quit," she said aloud. "Stop agonizing." She grinned. First it had been thoughts of pregnancy and babies, now dissatisfaction with her job. Was that what they meant by a biological clock?

More likely, she thought as she headed down the hall, she just had a bad case of infatuation, which time would undoubtedly heal.

Samantha, when Maggie looked in on her, had fallen asleep over her studies. Maggie gently removed the book and turned out the light, then flipped the quilt over her. For a moment, she looked at her daughter tenderly, seeing in memory all the Samanthas she had tucked in through the years. Now Sam was nearly a woman, but her face still showed the faintest traces of the little girl she had been.

Joel was propped on the porch railing when she came out. "Done so fast?"

She shook her head. "I didn't get it done." She sat on the swing on his end of the porch and kicked it into a sway. "No motivation."

"Maybe I can help," he suggested.

You've already done enough, she thought. "No, I'm just not with it tonight." She glanced at him, lifting her eyebrows quickly once to indicate resignation. "I'll do it tomorrow."

She definitely sounded blue, Joel thought. Beneath her eyes were shadows. He felt a pang of conscience. Tonight, he'd wanted her all to himself the instant he had seen her, and he'd used her physical attraction to him to draw her back outside with him.

Now he saw that she had a lot to think about. The newspaper took an enormous amount of time, especially given Maggie's devotion to detail. Rarely had he ever seen a misspelled word or a clumsy headline. Page designs were well balanced, and the photos were creative. Even the quality of news covered showed a good feeling for the readers themselves—not an easy feat for a woman ten to fifteen years older than they were.

She did it because she loved the kids, held a rare sympathy for their dramas and crises and need to be noticed. It showed in the solid relationship she had developed with Sam, who spoke of Maggie with a deep respect balanced with teasing humor.

He took a seat on the swing next to her and put his arm around her. "Come here," he said quietly. She rested her head on his shoulder with a sigh. Gently, he pressed his cheek against her hair and with slow, easy movements, massaged her shoulders.

For a long time, they sat there together without speaking, the swing rocking back and forth in the cool evening. Joel held her pressed to his chest, smelling the scent of her shampoo mixed with the smell of the night itself. Her body fit next to his as if they'd been carved from one piece of wood.

As she relaxed against him, he thought, finally, that everything had been worth it. If it had been necessary to undergo the struggles and dark years to reach this moment with Maggie in the mellow spring night, he would gladly endure them all again.

With the thought, he turned to press a kiss to her forehead—and grinned to himself. Maggie had fallen asleep, cradled in his arms.

She trusted him, like Moses did. The knowledge gave him a knife thrust of sorrow, for eventually, he would have to betray that trust. Moses asked nothing more than Joel's attention, the assurance of food and a warm place to sleep—things that must have been unimaginable to the old tom.

Like Moses, Maggie had survived long, cold nights and a ragged hunger—in her tales of her father, he could hear the lingering pain of an emotionally battered child. That her ex-husband had also betrayed her reinforced the belief she held that men were not to be trusted.

His chest tightened with guilt. Oh, Maggie, Maggie, he thought. I hope you'll find a way to forgive me when the moment comes.

It was wrong. He could see that now. But as he held her in his arms, he didn't see how he could give up— not yet. For if his gamble succeeded, they would both shed the chains of the past, and his debt would be paid.

Chapter Eight

Thursday afternoon Maggie groggily opened the door to her grandmother at the usual time. "Good afternoon," she said with a yawn.

"Thunderation, child," Anna said with concern, "you look ready for the hospital."

Maggie kissed the cool, powdered cheek. "I'm okay, Gram. Just worked late last night." She padded into the kitchen in her robe. Once there, she blinked, trying to remember what she'd been about to do. Oh, coffee. Right.

"I'll take care of that," Anna said, taking the filters and coffee can from Maggie's hands. "I'd tell you to go back to bed, but I know you won't do it, so just sit down and have a bear claw."

The bear claws didn't look very appealing, for once. Maggie rubbed her face. Weariness weighed on her.

Her grandmother frowned. "Why don't you take a vacation?"

"I'll be all right," Maggie said. "There's just been a lot going on lately. I never seem to get it all done." To prove to her grandmother that she was fine, she served herself a bear claw and began to choke it down.

Her statement was only partially true. Her life had been extremely busy lately, with shortages of help at the paper, the need to get Samantha ready for her trip to Denver and the constant extra work created by the Proud Fox conflict. But her exhaustion stemmed from a lack of sleep—and she hadn't lain awake at night haunted by those worries.

She couldn't get Joel Summer off her mind.

She also had no one to discuss her feelings with. There was no one who would understand why she was afraid of him. What, after all, could she say was wrong with him, except that she was frightened by the deeply passionate nature she sensed below his playfulness? And that he had some painful things to work through, things he wasn't willing to show Maggie? As he'd said, time would help them know each other better.

But he frightened her in a way no man ever had. Just being with him released all the careful holds she'd kept over herself all these years.

Galen, she thought suddenly. Galen would understand. She would call him tonight.

"Maggie," Anna said, sitting down with two fresh cups of coffee, "I hate to bring this up, but I think you need to know that some of the church is angry at the way you're covering this rock band problem."

Maggie straightened and reached for her cup. "That's their prerogative."

"You have to think of Samantha, too, you know."

"I am thinking of Samantha." She frowned. "Is there talk of keeping us out or something?"

"Not exactly." Anna's eyelids flickered down. "But a lot of people are pretty unhappy."

"Well, frankly, Gram, so am I." She leaned over the table, her fury rekindled. "Did you read the statistics about the riot at the ticket outlet? Seventeen kids injured. I think the whole thing has gone too far." She narrowed her eyes. "But you know what? I can't find out who's in charge of the kids who are protesting. No one will talk to me. It's beginning to seem a little weird.... Why aren't there adults in charge, putting a stop to the protest?"

Anna pursed her lips. "Maybe I can help you find out."

"If you can find anything, I'd appreciate it." Maggie pinched a bit of pastry and popped it into her mouth. "You know," she said after a minute, "I guess it is possible that the kids just got together and decided to stage this by themselves." But she'd thought more and more lately, there was something slightly askew about the whole situation, something she felt she'd almost stumbled over several times. "I do know one thing. There's a boy named Cory who is supposed to be a spokesman or something. When I ask questions, that's whose name comes up."

"Do you know where he goes to school?"

Maggie shook her head. "I don't know anything about him."

"I'll talk to some people I know at the various churches." Anna touched her hand. "It's beginning to worry me, too."

"Thanks." Maggie smiled and turned the conversation to lighter things. "What about that great-granddaughter of yours, huh?" she said with a grin. "She made the front page of the city daily at the age of fifteen."

"Weren't you frightened for her?"

Maggie remembered the night, Samantha exuberantly shooting the action with no thought for safety. "Yes. But you wouldn't have stopped her, either. She's got her mama's blood in her veins, I think."

"Her mama died when Samantha was three."

"I know." Maggie cocked her head. "But a safe life isn't what everyone wants. I bet if you gave Samantha's mother the choice to live her life over again, she'd live it exactly the same way."

"Some people's work is that important to them." Anna smiled at Maggie.

"Exactly." Her appetite was returning, Maggie realized with pleasure. She selected a sticky bun, poured another cup of coffee and with a wicked smile said, "Come on, Gram. I want to know what they're saying about me at church."

"You little gossip," Anna chided. But she leaned forward, eager to laugh about the exaggerations.

Unfortunately, Galen was little help in understanding her reticence about Joel when Maggie spoke to him that night. Samantha had gone to a movie with David, who'd borrowed a car for the evening, and Maggie took advantage of the solitude to place her call.

"This guy sounds terrific, Maggie," Galen said. "I think I'd just let it unfold for a while. You don't have to marry him, you know."

At this, Maggie felt a flush of embarrassment. "It's not even a serious relationship or anything."

"You know, sis, I hate to say it, but you need to let yourself go a little bit. Trust him. Trust yourself."

"Oh, fine," she said with irritation. "I call you to be my champion, and you throw me right back there in the ring."

"Don't you get lonely?" he asked in a sober voice. "I do. I'm tired of doing it all myself. We both had a pretty rotten childhood, but it doesn't have to ruin the rest of our lives."

"At least I've sampled marriage. You're five years older than I am, and you've never even tried to get serious about anyone."

"Sure I have. I've tried, but Maggie, I don't think I have the skills I need. You do."

For the first time, Maggie understood that Galen had his own warped self-image to contend with. At the very thought of her sensitive, handsome brother lacking the skills to keep a marriage together, she smiled, but changed the subject. He never dealt well with her insights into his personality—a remainder of the eldest brother mentality, she supposed. "When are you coming to see me?"

"I can't say exactly, but I'm hoping for late June. Is that good for you?"

"Sure. I'll stock up."

"Great. Hang in there, kid."

"Thanks."

As she hung up, Maggie shook her head. "Some help you were," she said aloud, staring darkly out the kitchen window. It was a few minutes past sunset, and the backyard was outlined in the silvery, soft light of dusk. The lilacs glowed an unearthly shade of pale purple, and Maggie knew just how they would smell. All at once, her bad mood dropped away and she headed outdoors.

Settled on the picnic bench, her skirt draped over her knees, a shawl over her shoulders, she let her worries fade with the day. She didn't brood by nature, simply because it was too hard to resist the small joys she found in moments just like these. As she sat there on the hard wooden bench, she realized she probably wouldn't feel so panicked over her attraction to Joel if his appearance in her life hadn't coincided with both Samantha's annual trek to see her father and the chaos in her working life. She'd been so tired the past week that she'd found the barest thought processes difficult.

So she let her thoughts wander where they would, watching the sky deepen from dust to night.

When Joel soundlessly joined her in the cove made by the lilac bushes, she was able to look up at him with pleasure. "Hi," she said.

He settled next to her on the bench and took her hand. "Hi."

They said nothing at all for a long time, listening together to the crickets whirring in the grass. From several blocks away came the sound of traffic, engines and horns and tires, pleasantly muted. Children down the street called farewells to friends as mothers gathered them in. A breeze floated over Maggie's face, sweet and heavy with lilacs, and her hand in Joel's was comfortable and warm.

"One of my birds died today," Joel said after a long time.

"Oh, I am sorry," Maggie said, turning. In her serene mood, it seemed no trouble to offer sympathy. "Do you want to tell me about him?"

He looked at her for a minute, then lifted her hand and kissed the knuckles. "Yes," he said. "I think I do."

And so he did. It was a simple story. A red-tailed hawk, its wing torn off when it tangled with a barbed wire fence, had failed to recover after an amputation.

"The thing that makes me sad," Joel said in his gravelly voice, "is that there wasn't any physical reason for him to die. He just gave up."

"If he had lived, he wouldn't have flown."

Joel nodded. His eyes swept the sky in the curiously familiar gesture Maggie had noted before. After a moment, he said, "I really liked that bird."

With her free hand, she reached up to touch his clean jaw, turning his face to hers.

"Silly to get worked up over a bird, isn't it?" he said with a rueful smile.

"No," she said quietly. "It makes you all the more human."

He touched her chin with one finger. "I wish I'd met you when I was twenty," he said, and kissed her.

Maggie didn't resist as he slanted his mouth down hard on hers, using his free hand to cup her head as he sought comfort. And as she met the force of his kiss, she knew instinctively that he needed solace for more than the death of the bird—the secrets that lived in his eyes were tormenting him, as well. With a calm sense of release, Maggie realized she didn't need to know the sorrows to address them.

She let her hand open on his face, feeling the feathery point where his eyelashes met and the pulse in his temple. As his lips moved, so did the tiny muscles in his cheek and jaw. Maggie reveled in all of it—the combination of his lips on hers, his face against her palm, his fingers tangled in her hair.

As the kiss deepened, he let her hand go and lifted her with powerful arms onto his lap. With almost desperate hunger, his tongue explored her mouth, urged hers to enter his. She explored the terrain of his neck and shoulders, moving her fingers into the coarse, full hair, then down under the collar of his shirt to the heated skin.

He used one great arm to brace her against his broad chest, and with the other hand, caressed her arm, then circled her neck as if gauging its width and finally, moved through her hair. Maggie felt an electric passion begin to glow in her nerves, a breathless anticipation in her chest.

When he let his hand slide open over her neck and collarbone, toward the bodice of her buttoned blouse, she shivered in anticipation, and there was no thought in her mind of stopping him.

Instead, as his hand moved to her buttons, hers fell on his, and they worked as a team, loosening garments. When his shirt was open, Maggie eagerly ran her hand over the rippling chest, her fingers spiraling with pleasure over the hard-muscled rises covered with crisp hair. His lips bruised hers, and a growl of hunger sounded in his throat.

When Maggie rubbed the tiny nipples on his chest, feeling them harden against the friction, Joel tore his mouth from hers and burned a path over her neck. In turn, she bit his shoulder, overwhelmed with the joyous burst of passion consuming her. Never had anything felt as good as this, she thought dazedly. Beneath her, pressing into her thigh with more power than she would have believed possible, his arousal insisted it was no different for Joel.

He pushed her almost roughly into the hollow of his elbow, his fingers raking over her bra. As he released the closure, exposing her breasts to the cool, lilac-scented night, he paused, and Maggie with him, on the brink of something unutterably magnificent. Her hands ceased and a violent trembling rocked her body as she waited, feeling his eyes upon her naked breasts.

Suddenly he descended, his huge, dark head falling to her breasts. Maggie gasped as the lips that had so expertly kissed her now performed an exquisite craft of arousal of another sort. "You taste like morning," he whispered, suckling softly, "and dew." His mouth lazily circled her breasts, then he kissed the place between. "Like all the sunbeams that ever danced."

He lifted his head to take her lips again, pressing their bared chests together. Holding her tightly, he said quietly, "I want you, Maggie." He nuzzled her shoulder and sighed. "But there are things I need to tell you."

"You will, when it's time," she said, pressing her forehead against his neck. "Don't torture yourself in the meantime."

He growled happily, squeezing her.

Shifting away, Maggie managed to fasten her bra and buttons once more, then rebuttoned Joel's shirt. When it was done, she cocked her head. "It's strange how comfortable I am with you."

With a gentle hand, he smoothed her hair away from her forehead. "Must be that other life."

She smiled. "Must be." For a few minutes more, they lingered, holding each other in the sweet night. Then Maggie sighed. "I really have a lot of work to do. I have to go in."

"I won't keep you, then." Grasping her firmly around the waist, he stood up and swung her around before setting her on the ground.

"You love playing Tarzan, don't you?" she said, brushing her clothes back into place.

"As long as you're Jane." He kissed her quickly.

Maggie laughed, then stood on tiptoes to kiss him. "And I love that—feeling small."

A sudden crash broke the still night. Whirling toward the house, Maggie said, "What was that?"

"We'd better check," Joel answered grimly, shoving her aside as he took the lead on the path around the house.

As Maggie trailed behind, she was struck with the change in him. He moved with stealth and speed, cloaked with a definite aura of dangerous power. It reminded her of the night they'd met on the front porch, when he'd nearly crouched at the unexpected noise of the swing creaking. Where had he learned to be so wary? Nothing in the childhood stories he'd shared with her suggested danger, nor did she think life at a university would be fraught with unexpected pitfalls.

They rounded the front silently, surprising two teens in black leather who were spray painting the sidewalk. Maggie stared at them in dismay for a split second, wondering how to best handle the situation. Joel indulged no such hesitation. He sprung from the shadows alongside the porch, like a leopard leaping from a tree. It was a gesture so smooth and effortless, Maggie felt her breath catch. The speed wasn't quite enough to snag the intruders, however. They raced away instantly, chains jingling, and were lost to the night.

Belatedly, Maggie joined Joel, who stared at the painted sidewalk with a frown. "Look at this," he said.

Scrawled in black paint on the concrete were odd symbols, together with the words Long Live Proud Fox. "What are those things?" she asked.

"That's a pentagram and I'm not sure what the other is, but it's associated with devil worship."

"Devil worship?" Maggie repeated, bewildered.

"Does Proud Fox write music that could be interpreted that way?"

Maggie shook her head. "Not at all." She folded her arms. "I've objected to their music because of the way they reinforce the idea that drugs and drunkenness are glorious—some kind of alternative to a dead-end life." She'd studied the lyrics of the band exhaustively. "There are even references to God as a kind of sorrowing figure. Nothing like this."

Joel narrowed his eyes and meditatively looked down the street. In his stance, Maggie saw lingering traces of the dangerous aura he'd assumed. A ripple of amazement at his physical power traveled through her as she stared at him, perplexed. Who are you, Joel Summer? she thought. For the first time, his hidden past was a little disturbing.

He touched her arm. "Let's go see if there's anything else inside."

"Inside?"

"Look at your front window."

Maggie turned. Her curtains billowed out on a current of wind, the fabric catching on corners of jagged glass. "Terrific," Maggie said with a tsk, and headed for the house. "This has all gone far enough. I'm tired of it."

"We need to call the police."

"You'd better believe it." She paused with her hand on the door, cocking her head. "It just occurred to me I have a valuable source I haven't used at all," she said. David would know if there had been plans to vandalize her home. Whether he would tell or not remained to be seen—but unless she'd seriously misjudged the boy, he wouldn't approve of this kind of violence. "I'm going to get to the bottom of this."

Joel measured her for a moment. "I hope you'll be careful."

The next morning, Joel entered the mews where healing and permanent resident birds were housed. The enclosure was made entirely of redwood and divided into spacious cages. In all, several dozen birds could be accommodated. Presently, forty-two birds lived in the mews, all raptors, ranging from gigantic bald eagles and turkey vultures to tiny screech owls. As Joel made his way down the graveled path between the two halves of the building, he spoke to each of the birds by name, pausing at the cage of a bald eagle who'd been permanently injured four years ago. Named Quanah after the mixed-blood Comanche chief, the eagle had thrived in the center, making peace with his limited surroundings with a rare grace. As Joel stood in front of his quarters, Quanah lifted his head and croaked in greeting, the high, weak call oddly appealing from such a fierce-looking bird.

"Good dreams of the old days, Quanah?" Joel said with a smile. "There are kids coming today—thought you might want to practice looking ferocious."

The eagle ruffled his shoulder feathers, croaking as if in disappointment. Across the way, a great horned owl hooted. Around its ankles was a restraining device to keep it from flying, and it glowered at Joel when he glanced over. "Won't be long now, Jeremiah. You'll see."

The owl blinked and Joel laughed. He joined a dark-haired woman in the cubicle of a golden eagle. "Is she ready?" Joel asked.

The woman grinned. "Chomping at the bit."

The eagle, recovered from a gunshot wound to the shoulder, moved toward Joel in anticipation. Around her leg was a jess, a leather thong used in the ancient art of falconry—training hawks to hunt. Joel took the attached leash in his left hand and offered his right arm, securely covered with a thick leather glove, to the bird. She climbed on immediately, grasping the leather with long talons. With a noble straightening of her feathers, she looked toward the door.

"I love this part," Joel said.

He carried the eagle outside to the yellow field surrounding the mews. The bird's alert eyes swept the landscape and the sky with an eagerness that matched Joel's.

He let her fly on the leash in a few circles, to test the analysis he'd made two days before. Her wing was strong again, with no weakness or favoring. She'd flown on the leash for hours the other day with no problems.

She returned to his arm, the talons making a scratching sound against the leather. For one moment, Joel admired her red-gold feathers and noble head, the penetrating dark eyes and hooked beak. Then he took the jess from her ankle and lifted his arm. "A long life to you, beauty."

The eagle flapped powerful wings to gain altitude, then circled above him. Joel watched her test the wind currents and the feel of her unfettered freedom. She called loudly, as if in farewell, then rose high and sailed away.

He felt, as he watched her, a tightness in his chest, a swell of gratitude and joy so great he could hardly contain it. This was the moment he had missed most desperately in the dark years, the moment when a recovered bird could take to the sky once again. It reinforced his belief that man could be a friend to the earth and all her creatures and brought home the pattern of his own life.

At his feet, Joel saw one long tail feather. He stooped to pick it up. The honeyed color was just the shade of Maggie's hair. As he looked at it, he thought he'd like to bring her here, show her these birds. Perhaps then she might understand a little more of him.

He sighed. The situation was growing more and more complicated. As he'd mapped out his plan in those first days of freedom, it had all come together so clearly. He'd been unable to foresee the violent chemistry that had bloomed instantly between them. If he'd ever imagined her at all, it was as a plain but pleasing woman who'd be good company for him if they could form a normal kind of relationship on the outside. It was enough for him that they'd shared such a close alliance on a mental level.

His only reason for hiding his past in the beginning had been to give her space to accept or reject him as she would any other man. Somehow, that had backfired, and now he felt trapped in a lie he'd never intended to perpetuate. Last night, he'd seen the speculation in her eyes over the change in him—it had frightened her.

Still absorbed in his thoughts, he wandered back into the mews. "Now what?" he asked Quanah. Had he gone too far already to confess his lie? Would it be better to tell her now, get it done, accept the consequences? Or should he wait a bit longer, until he knew her love had grown strong enough to survive the blow?

What if it never grew that strong? his conscience prodded. The thought made him feel breathless.

Samantha's summer gear was loaded into Paul's Mercedes, the crowd had been fed, and now they all gathered on the porch to say goodbye.

As she joined the others, Maggie felt the pull of loneliness. Looking at David, she knew he felt the same thing, and she touched his arm gently as she stepped forward. Anna hugged Sam hard. "You be good, sugar."

"I will, Gram."

Paul, an elegant, slim man in his forties, cleared his throat, rattling his keys in a restless manner that Maggie hated. Ignoring him, she took her turn with Sam, keeping her farewell hug as brief as possible. Although Sam would be gone just six weeks, Maggie chose not to intrude on Paul's time with his daughter, and this was the last she'd see of Sam until the end of July—unless Galen came. The thought enabled her to pull back. "Have a good time, sweetie—but be good. Your dad has enough gray hair as it is."

"I'll miss you, Mom . . ." Sam whispered. "I'll call every Saturday."

"I'll be here."

Samantha looked at David. Constrained by the adults around them, they were forced to say goodbye with hands and eyes. David touched the golden broken heart on a chain around Sam's neck, and she touched his. They said not a word. "I'll start my first letter today," she finally said softly.

"Me, too." David let go of her and swallowed. Watching them, Maggie was deeply touched.

"Bye, everybody," Sam said, heading over the blackened sidewalk toward the car. Unable to remove the ugly marks, Maggie had spray painted over them.

A whistle, bright and clear, sounded from down the street. Maggie glanced up to see Joel, riding hard on his ten-speed toward them. Under his arm was a brown bag. Samantha waved at him and he let go of the handlebars to straighten and wave. Maggie smiled wryly to herself. He was an irrepressible show-off sometimes.

He guided the bike into a driveway and rode up to the knot of people at the end of the sidewalk, delivering the brown paper bag into Samantha's hands. "Glad I caught you," he said.

Sam peaked inside. "Photography magazines!" she exclaimed. "Thanks, Joel," she said, beaming.

Paul met Maggie's eyes in question. Maggie cleared her throat and stepped forward. "Joel," she said, "this is Samantha's father, Paul Henderson. Paul, this is—um—my neighbor Joel Summer."

The two men shook hands uneasily. Next to Joel, Paul looked like a slender sapling. A sapling, she thought with a repressed smile, that had been deprived of good sunlight. Though he traveled ceaselessly to exotic locales in his career as a photographer, his tan looked somehow sallow next to the vigorous good health Joel exuded like a personal scent.

"I have dinner reservations for us this evening, Samantha. We need to get rolling," Paul said. "Take care, Maggie." He kissed the top of her head.

They departed amid waves and shouts. Anna pleaded church commitments and headed for her car, leaving Joel, Maggie and David standing on the blackened pavement like misarranged chess pieces. "I'll see ya," David mumbled.

Maggie stopped him with one hand on his shoulder. "I'll be missing her, too," she said. "Come by for dinner or something sometimes, okay?"

His pale eyes lightened with relief, and he gave her a wry grin. "I will, Mrs. Henderson." He paused, bit his lip. "I might also know something about your story sometime soon."

"Good. Thanks."

He ambled off with carefully careless strides.

Maggie turned toward Joel and found him heading toward the porch with his bike. An emptiness pinched her chest. It had seemed the past week as if he'd been avoiding her. Had she misread his signals that night in the lilac bushes? She bit her lip. No. She might be somewhat inexperienced with men, but she knew he'd wanted her that night. Affecting a casual attitude, she followed him back to the porch. "It's always hard when she leaves for the summer," she said in opening.

He half smiled as he bent to secure a chain around his bike wheels. "I'll miss her, too."

"Would you like to have a cup of coffee with me?"

Joel stood, rubbing one hand against his jeans with a curiously nervous gesture. "I have some paperwork I need to get done," he said.

Maggie looked at him for a minute, then backed toward her door, nodding. "Maybe another time."

"Yeah," he said. "Thanks."

Maggie fled into her living room and closed the door on the cloudy afternoon, her face burning with embarrassment. What had she done? His mood with Samantha had been cheerful, but as soon as she'd approached him, a wall had slammed into place.

When the worst of her mortification had passed, Maggie went to the kitchen to begin cleaning the mess left from lunch. As she stacked plates and sorted silverware, she wandered back over the time she'd spent with Joel, especially the night last week in the backyard. It had seemed, to her at least, a turning point.

But this entire week, he'd been scarce. She had seen him working in the garden, had heard his music playing and watched him come and go. Once, she'd been on her way outside to speak with him, and he'd headed straight for his door, even though Maggie had been certain that he'd seen her.

She scrubbed a pan with unnecessary force. Chances were, she'd simply pegged him wrong—he'd only *seemed* sincere. He was probably a charmer, after all.

The trouble with that picture was that a charming man, seeing the goal of seducing Maggie nearly complete, would not back away but rather forge ahead with gusto.

Damn. She peeled her rubber gloves off with a sense of confusion and frustration. At the moment, she'd prefer a charmer. Somewhere in the past week, she'd ceased to care if she ever found a flaw in Joel. She didn't care what he was hiding. She didn't mind that he kindled within her a passion she feared was dangerous and perhaps unhealthy.

She wanted him with every beat of her heart. A restlessness dogged her steps every moment that she couldn't be with him; it crawled under her skin and kept her from sleeping.

Thus far, she'd managed to keep herself from analyzing the emotion too deeply for fear of what she would find. And she didn't allow much now, only an admission that she not only liked and respected Joel Summer, but she definitely wanted to share his bed— right or wrong.

Was it wrong? If it wasn't, would she have held off in Samantha's presence?

Her wandering gaze caught on the framed photograph that Samantha had had published in the city daily. Sam had a rich future awaiting her—and Maggie had done almost everything she could do to make sure her daughter would make the right choices when adulthood overtook her. From here on out, Maggie's role would consist of being there for Samantha to lean on as she began to decide her life.

Therein lay the trouble, Maggie thought. For ten years, her life had been centered upon Samantha—and she regretted not a whit of it. But now, her own needs were clamoring for satisfaction. It was time for her to acknowledge them. No, she didn't take lovers lightly. But a grown woman could form responsible alliances with men similarly inclined.

Thus fortified, Maggie straightened her shoulders, found her jacket—and headed for her car. After all, in the absence of courage, there was always work.

Chapter Nine

As afternoon deepened into evening, a hard rain began to fall. Maggie had worked with dedication for several hours, but the gray storm stole the last of her motivation. She locked up the newspaper office firmly and headed home, planning to view a movie she'd rented from the video store and eat everything in sight.

But when she reached the top stair of her porch, her feet carried her to Joel's door instead of her own, and her hand lifted itself to knock with a good deal of authority on the screen door. Beyond the sound of the pattering rain, she heard his music.

A fit of panic slammed into her chest. What if he was entertaining another woman? There had been no signs of one in his life, but one never knew—perhaps that was the reason he'd seemed distant. She dipped her head, trying to think of a reason for knocking. A cup of sugar—that was a time-tried, but worthy, excuse. Mentally, she rehearsed her lines.

When Joel swung open the door, wearing a sleeveless T-shirt the color of his incredible eyes, her lines fled. She swallowed. "Can I come in?" she blurted out.

Casually, he pushed open the screen. "Sure."

Maggie brushed the wet from her jacket, then took it off and stepped inside, smelling coffee. The air inside was moist and warm, and the sound of a mournful ballad playing on the stereo added a smoky atmosphere. "I hope I'm not interrupting your dinner," she said.

"No." He shifted a stack of books from the couch to the coffee table. "Have a seat."

Gingerly, Maggie settled on the edge of the couch, her hands folded in her lap. Now what? Moses circled around her legs, and she reached down to pet his glossy back.

Joel settled in one of the chairs by the window. He said nothing.

Maggie took in the thick fall of hair over his high forehead, his blunt nose and full lips. In his huge hands, he shifted a paperback book back and forth restlessly.

"You're sending me mixed messages, Joel," she said finally. She forced herself to meet his eyes. "I don't know how to act when you do that. I can live with it if you've changed your mind and don't want to see me, but I'd like to know."

Joel looked at her. Her tiger eyes glowed as if they held their own light, and her hair was slightly damp with rain, her skin dewy with its mist. He put the book down and crossed the room, unable to resist the lure of her honest confusion or the promise of the harbor she offered. "Changed my mind?" he echoed with an ironic note. He took her hand and tugged her to her feet. "You act like there was a choice involved."

He crushed her against him, feeling a sweet explosion as their bodies met—hers strong but rounded against his, her solid height filling his arms, covering a lifetime of cold places. As she melted against him, he let go of everything but the moment, unable to resist her unguarded coming.

Upon his mouth, her hair felt heavy and smelled of rain. Her breasts thrust against his chest, and he let his hands wander over the dip of her spine to the full swell of her bottom, allowing the generous flesh to fill his hands for a moment before he pulled her more tightly into him.

He nudged away the hair over her ear and tasted the spare arc of skin at her earlobe, suckling gently until she sagged against him. At that instant, Joel felt her hands slip under his T-shirt in the back, and her cold fingertips ran up the length of him. He nipped her earlobe and heard her laugh with throaty enjoyment.

All the desire that had been building within him now slowly filled every molecule of his body with the realization that it was Maggie, his sweet, sweet Maggie, in his arms. He tightened his hold. "I won't let you go this time," he growled, and took her lips with a nearly unbearable hunger—a hunger deeper than anything physical, one unlike anything he'd ever known. With Maggie in his arms he felt whole, as if all the worn, raveled wounds of his soul were being healed.

Maggie drank of him, opening her lips to his seeking, searing tongue. Her arms looped hard around his neck. Her feet barely touched the floor as one of his arms anchored her waist against his body.

A fierce desire swept through her, as if all the vivid imaginings she'd indulged since meeting him had narrowed to this moment in his arms. "Make love to me, Joel," she murmured, and raked her fingernails lightly down his sides.

He groaned and Maggie thrilled to the evidence of his arousal pressed against her belly. His mouth bruised hers in dizzying promise. "You know I want you," he said against her lips. "But I'm not prepared."

Maggie dipped her head shyly and whispered, "That's okay." Then, lifting her eyes to his, she added, "I am."

His grin was dazzling. He scooped her up into his arms. Maggie gasped as he headed for the steps that led upstairs.

"I can walk," she protested. "I was only kidding about Tarzan."

He dipped to kiss her as he took the first stair. "I'm not taking any chances." He grinned, his dimples showing deeply. "I've always wanted to do this. Don't deprive me."

His voice rumbled through his chest and into her body, and Maggie laughed at the sheer delight of being carried—actually carried—by a man.

He made his way down the hall to the twin of her own bedroom. The room was dark with rain and evening. Just beyond the threshold, he paused, still cradling her, to press his lips to hers. "You can't imagine how many times I've heard you moving next door and wanted to tear the wall down." He moved to the small alcove off the bedroom and settled her upon a mattress covered with a thick quilt and an assortment of oversize pillows. The cool scent of rain wafted in through an open window.

Maggie knelt and drew Joel down to face her. She opened her palms to spread her fingers upon his face. "You weren't alone," she breathed, tasting his sculpted mouth once more, "in wanting to tear down the wall." With bold but unhurried movements, she ran her tongue over the unfamiliar corners of his lips, letting it dart toward his teeth and the thrust of his tongue. His was a flavor unlike any she'd ever known, not sweet or salty. He tasted of himself, like a summer sky, like a bird in flight.

His hands moved from her hips up over her ribs with agonizing slowness, until they nearly covered her from the lower swell of her breasts to her shoulders. "I'm sorry about this week," he murmured, tasting the flesh of her neck. "I must have been crazy to think—"

"Shh," Maggie whispered. "It doesn't matter now."

"You're beautiful, Maggie," he breathed, letting his fingers slide down over the hard tips of her breasts. There he paused to play a light tattoo that sent a quickening through her belly. She moaned softly.

Without hurry, he released each of the buttons on her shirt until it lay unfastened but closed over her.

"I've waited so long for this," he whispered, and at the heat in his eyes, Maggie felt a surge of power, the ancient power women have felt over their men for time immemorial. She waited.

He stretched out his fingers to slide the fabric aside, off her breasts, and for a long, endless time, simply moved his hands over the bared flesh. "Ah," he breathed at last, bending over her, "you are a sight to behold."

Gathering a supple breast into each hand, his tongue reached out to flitter over one, then the other, the moist touch no more than the errant tap of a moth's wing. The rasp of his skin grated the tender flesh as his head moved with his languid supping. She arched at the exquisite sensation.

Still Joel teased, curling his tongue around each gentle slope and rise, moving up to taste the hollow of her throat before slipping down once more.

All at once, he sucked one nipple into his mouth to roll it between his lips, and Maggie cried out, grasping his head between her breasts. He refused to let go, teasing and tasting and nibbling until Maggie thought she would explode.

A low, satisfied half laugh rumbled in his chest, and with a surge of joy, Maggie understood that he could play while they made love. It needn't be a rushed or serious thing—the night, at last, belonged to them.

"My turn," she murmured in his moment of laughter. She pushed him onto his back, flung her shirt away, and throwing her hair out of her eyes with a wicked grin, straddled him.

Until that moment, Joel had managed to maintain a semblance of control—he wanted to learn the terrain of her slowly, to savor every inch of her. As she knelt over him, her breasts free and glistening, her hair tumbling like tawny velvet around her naked shoulders, he felt his control snap.

She leaned down and took his lips, tasting him the way he'd tasted her. "Too bad," she teased, "that you aren't wearing buttons I could tear off."

"Allow me," he said, half sitting to twist his shirt off in one quick motion, then falling back to the bed. He reached to touch her again, reveling in the contrast of his work-roughened hands against her pliant breasts. Her hips moved alluringly over his, her hair brushed his cheek and her nipples burned with hard heat into his palms.

Her fingers traced his shoulders and chest, and as they moved, Joel felt her mood shift. Her voice was breathless, constricted when she spoke. "Joel," she said, bending to press her lips to the places her fingers had learned, "you're so incredible I can hardly believe you're real."

"I'm real," he assured her, gathering her to him. "You're the wraith. You've bewitched me."

He laid her gently upon the quilt and stripped away her jeans and underwear, then shed his own. When he would have stretched next to her, Maggie knelt and urgently held him away, unable to resist admiring him in the rain-dimmed light. In reverence, she let her hands rove over the tight curve of his shoulders, trace the wide triangle of black hair on his chest, revel in the might and breadth of his rib cage. With her mouth, she tasted the curve of his bicep.

At last, she swayed forward to let her unclothed body brush his, feeling an overwhelming swell of delight at the long-sought press of him against her. His breath rasped against her shoulder, her breasts met his magnificent chest—and Maggie sighed. The sweetness was so acute, she could have knelt that way with him for the rest of her life, reveling in the joy of the simple contact of their bodies.

But Joel was not so content. His hands roamed her, traveling over thighs and belly and neck, as if he wanted to memorize the feel of her. And as his hands and lips roved and teased and explored, Maggie knew that she, too, must find release in his arms. The thought gave her a brief moment of terror, and as his gentle fingers approached the deep center of her womanhood, his hands nudging her thighs apart, she froze.

"There's a tiger waiting in your eyes, love," he whispered. "Let me unleash it." His voice rumbled almost below register. "I won't hurt you."

The ministrations he offered were too gentle to resist. Maggie let go, gave herself to Joel, to the man
who'd captured her like a kite on a string. And like the
kite, he held her loosely while she gained altitude,
reined her in when she would have plunged, fed her
more line to let her soar until she felt herself hovering
high above the earth, connected only by the touch of
his hand to anything remotely real. She cried his name,
begging him to come to her.

And at last, he plunged with her, in her, with restraint and power. As he thrust, Maggie felt herself
soar through a bank of clouds into a burst of golden
light, blinding and utterly dazzling. She arched and
gasped, riding the currents of Joel until she knew he,
too, had met the sky. His mouth closed upon hers, and
the light grew and exploded.

They drifted slowly back to earth together. Maggie
opened her eyes to find his fixed upon her face, his
sorrow gone. In its place glowed a transcendent
beauty, the same gloriously beautiful light Maggie had
seen upon his face the day he'd spoken of the red-
tailed hawk that had begun his career. This time, she
dared to reach for him, letting her fingers worship his
magnificent face.

Making a warm, purring sound, she sighed. "Well,
Tarzan, I think you found your tiger."

With gentle hands, he cupped her face. "I knew you
were in there." Joel felt a tenderness and joy greater
than any he'd ever known. And with a touch of fear,
he knew the joining had gone deeper than either of
them could yet guess.

He wrapped her close to him, touching her body with as much of himself as he possibly could, and they dozed gently together, awaking to love and rest, love and rest all through the night.

At one point as they lay curled in the quilt, listening to the rain fall against the trees beyond the windows, Joel stroked Maggie's hair. She leaned into his chest, content to listen to the deep thudding of his heart below her ear. "Are you sure this was okay?" he asked softly.

"I am now." She cast around for a way to express herself. "That wasn't like anything that ever happened to me before."

"Me, either."

"Really?" She scanned his face for truth, feeling exposed and vulnerable in a way that was uncomfortable. "You don't have to say that. I mean, maybe I just don't know a lot about this. I've only..."

He grinned. "You've only what?"

"Nothing."

"You've only had one lover—maybe two?"

"One," she corrected. "I guess that makes me seem a little backward."

"Then we both are—me even more than you." He chuckled. "Being a man and all."

Maggie couldn't disguise her astonishment. "Your wife was your only lover?"

He half shrugged. "We met when I was fourteen. Not much time for anyone else."

She twisted her mouth. "I wonder why men think they have to be Casanovas? I hate that double standard, and I hate it both ways. If it's okay for a woman to make choices, it's okay for a man to have the same ones."

Joel slid a hand with ease over the sleek, tawny skin of her shoulder.

"Still," she said, smiling, "I'm proud and honored."

"And well you should be," he teased, dipping to kiss her. They returned with laughter into the cushion of the mattress, curling there until the night faded.

Morning found them both starved, and they carried coffee and bagels with cream cheese and jam outside to the picnic table in the backyard. Overhead, in merry celebration, a sparrow sang, flitting from branch to branch as a squirrel shook the best twigs. "Tell me about your wife, Joel," Maggie invited.

For an instant, Joel's eyes went cold. Then he lifted his cup, sipped the hot coffee carefully and put it down. "What do you want to know?"

Maggie shook her head. "I don't know. Was she pretty?"

"Like a rose—very lush and velvety at first." He swallowed, as if the memory gave him pain. "Her hard living showed pretty fast, though. All the velvet wore off."

"How long ago did you divorce?"

"Seven years."

"And you stayed celibate all that time?" Maggie burst out.

Joel lifted his eyebrows with a sultry grin. "I was waiting for you."

It was hard to tell if the words were meant to throw her off her subject or if he really meant them. Maggie glanced at her plate with a little laugh.

He took her hand. "Look at me, Maggie."

She complied. At the brilliance of the jeweled eyes, so bright in his dark face, she nearly bolted again, terrified at the emotions he called up in her.

"What happened to me with Nina was a long time ago," he said. "But there are long-range repercussions that I'm not ready to discuss yet." The entreaty and sorrow had returned, and Maggie hated herself for putting it back when it had receded. He kissed her fingers. "I will tell you. I promise."

"I'm sorry," she said. "I'm being nosy again."

"No," he replied firmly. "You're honest—and I'm afraid I'm not." He let her hand go with a sigh and stood up. "Ah, hell," he said, turning away.

Maggie jumped up with a suddenly urgent need to still him. "No." She pressed her lips to his. "I don't want to know, not ever. It can be yours."

He uttered an oath and clasped her to him. Lifting his head, he took her face into his hands. He kissed her. "I mean it when I say I've waited for you a long time." A bittersweet smile touched his eyes. "Just think, if we'd met fifteen years ago, we'd both have saved a divorce."

"But I'd have missed Samantha."

He nodded his agreement and wrapped his arms around her, closing his eyes. As she returned the hug, he sent out a silent prayer. *Please, God, just give us a little time.*

Whatever she said about keeping his secret to himself, he knew the fabric of his untruth would come unraveled, leaving him exposed. But for the first time, he wondered if there might be a gentler way of showing her, a way to ease from lies to truth without shattering this new and vulnerable beauty enveloping them.

He would show her, carefully and slowly, who he was. Lifting his head, he pressed a kiss to her forehead. "Would you like to see my birds?"

Maggie had seen Joel in many attractive modes—riding his bike, thighs pumping with power; laughing and teasing as the moon rose over Colorado Springs; standing proud and naked before her last night, as perfect as Michelangelo's *David*. As she watched him work a falcon in the warm afternoon, however, all other visions paled.

As he worked Maggie could imagine him performing the same act in centuries long past. In her mind's eye, she saw the dark chestnut hair grown to the shoulders of a heavy leather vest, his stout, strong thighs encased in well-woven linen. His realm would have been thick forests; his power born of the deep link between himself and his fierce birds.

The vivid thought exhilarated her, sent her heart soaring for the heavens once more, without even touching him. Oh, Lord, she thought, I've gone and done it. Fallen head over heels, passionately in love.

The thought left her anxious for one long moment. Her parents had been ruined by passionate love, and it had already cast a pall over Joel's life.

But nothing this radiant, this powerful, could be wrong. When Joel motioned her to join him, she went eagerly, honored to share with him whatever portions of his life he could show her.

The falcon itself was a surprise, for she'd expected, somehow, an evil bird, huge and fierce. To the contrary, the prairie falcon was not much larger than a raven. Its face, wreathed in black, brown and cream feathers, was small and sweet, with enormous dark eyes that gave it a childlike expression. When Joel donned a leather glove, she noticed the long, sharp talons and hooked beak and realized its soft appearance cloaked powerful shoulders and wings tailored for incredible speed.

It was midway through recovery, Joel explained. A wildlife officer had found him in a sinkhole, and though the injuries couldn't really be explained, the bird had wrenched enough muscles and torn enough flesh to have been incapacitated for several months.

Like his medieval counterpart, Joel restrained the bird with a leather thong. For a time, it seemed content to ride on Joel's arm, eyes darting around the field with alert interest. With some nudging, it flew a little here and there, once making a swooping dance through the air to snag a mouse, which it promptly deposited at Joel's feet.

Joel grinned at the bird. "Thank you." With a complete lack of revulsion, he bent to snatch the mouse up by the tail, tossing it into the air. "You may have it."

The falcon swooped and snatched the carcass out of thin air, landing on the ground to devour the meal. Maggie turned away. "Sorry," she said, "but yuck."

"It's a good sign for this guy," Joel commented. "He's getting much stronger." He smiled at her. "We've had some great luck in the past month—I think the birds want to get out while there's plenty of youthful prey."

Maggie made a face. At Joel's tolerant, teasing smile, she defended herself. "I can't help it. Seems violent."

"They never kill except to eat or in defense of their young." His eyes darted out to the horizon. "Unlike man."

She nodded, thinking suddenly of her father, a professional soldier. She'd always considered him hawkish. Now, with a strange clarity she saw that his only flaw—though it had been a terrible one—had been his inability to draw distinctions between the laws of war and the laws of home.

Disturbed, she sighed. Lately, she wasn't sure what she thought about anything anymore.

Next to her, Joel laughed at the falcon, the sound rich and deep. In the sunlight his thick hair shone with ebony and chestnut and his eyes glittered with good cheer. He had upset her life, and yet, he was the one thing she was sure of. The paradox of it made her smile. "I'm hungry enough to eat that mouse myself," she said, touching his arm. "How about heading for the store sometime soon?"

Joel grinned, a sultry edge to his full lips. "By all means," he said, his gaze dropping to her mouth. His voice deepened. "I'll feed you whatever you like."

Maggie reached out to playfully run her hand over his thigh.

"Maybe," he murmured, "we ought to forget about eating and move directly to dessert."

She laughed and danced away from him. "You'd better concentrate on getting that bird home."

Handicapped by the bird on the jess, Joel couldn't follow his instincts, which dictated that he take her here in this deserted field with all the hurry and power he'd controlled last night. But he promised himself, as he took Maggie in with a glance, that he wouldn't put it off for more than an instant past his obligation.

Chapter Ten

Spring deepened into a mountain summer as the days of June passed swiftly. Maggie watched the lilacs fade for another year and roses take their place. Joel's garden of seedlings grew into sturdy plants in neat rows. The kitten that Moses had brought home was released from the prison of his cast and spent his days frolicking through the long grass in the backyard.

Like the season, Maggie felt herself ripen and bloom under the spell of her love for Joel. He, too, seemed to thrive. Gone were the shadows in his eyes—he laughed and teased with Maggie, playing practical jokes with a vengeance. Once it was a rubber spider, hung on a slender thread from the sun visor in her car—a joke that sent Maggie screaming when she climbed into the car one morning. Through the open door of his apartment, she heard Joel's booming laugh.

Another time, he borrowed David's leather and silver jacket, scrounged up a motorcycle from somewhere and took her cruising the main drags on Saturday night.

In return, Maggie cooked, astonishing herself with imaginative creations full of color and balance, which Joel consumed with a vigor that pleased her beyond all reckoning.

Although she would have been perfectly content in the first flush of love to let go of everything in the world unconnected to Joel, she did have to work. One morning, as Sharon and Maggie collaborated on the upcoming issue, Sharon said, "Are you actually humming?"

Maggie paused and flashed her friend a grin. "Guess I am."

"Mmm-hmm." Sharon shook her head. "He give you a class ring or anything yet?"

"A rubber spider," Maggie laughed, "and a six-pack of bubble gum. Do those count?"

Sharon grinned appreciatively. "I'm jealous."

"Maybe I'll keep my eyes peeled on your behalf."

"You know better than to try matchmaking, Maggie."

"Oh, I know." She grinned. "You should go out with my brother when he comes. You seemed to have hit it off the last time he was here. He's supposed to be in town any time now."

"We did have a good time the last time he was here." Sharon lifted an eyebrow wickedly. "Everywhere we went, the women wanted to chop me down and grab him for themselves. It was good for my ego."

"His, too." Maggie shook her head. Although Sharon and Galen were purely platonic friends, they'd clicked as well as Maggie and Sharon had. "You know, I don't think he has any idea how good-looking he is."

"That's impossible."

"No. He looks like my father, and because of the bad blood between them, I think Galen hates to look in the mirror."

"You look like your mom?"

Maggie shifted a ruler to count column inches on the page she was working on, then flashed a grin at Sharon. "Sure. Good looks run in the family."

"Oh, my, you've even gotten a little more confident," Sharon said with approval. "I like this guy better and better all the time."

"Seriously, why don't you come have dinner with us this week sometime?" The phone rang and Maggie put a hand on the receiver. "Think about it. We'd have a good time." Lifting the phone, she said "The *Wanderer*, Maggie speaking."

"Mrs. Henderson, it's David."

"Hi! What's up?" He'd been keeping her posted on the situation with the Proud Fox fans and the upcoming concert.

"There's gonna be trouble in Luther Park this morning. Thought you'd want to know."

"I'll be right there." She broke the connection and dialed the police, nodding to Sharon, who gathered her photo gear. "Possible trouble at Luther Park," Maggie said to the dispatch operator. She gave her name and details, then shoved a notebook into the voluminous pockets of her skirt. "Here we go again."

"I can't believe we can't find out who's behind these kids," Sharon said with irritation.

"One kid. That's all we need. I have a feeling that if we can find him, we can put all the rest together."

"We're running out of time." She blew a braid away from her face. "That concert's going to explode if somebody doesn't do something."

"Thank God Samantha is out of town," Maggie said.

Sharon drove with the expertise of a native of the Springs, her shortcuts and back roads cutting a full fifteen minutes off the time. The park scene was much the same as the others, a standoff of righteous indignation. The police had arrived by the time Maggie and Sharon pulled up, and the crowd was receding. Still, at the edges of the park, Maggie saw kids nursing minor wounds: a black eye, a split lip. Fistfighting, she thought.

As she stepped out of the car, she saw a boy running. On his jacket, in bright red, was a pentagram. Maggie took off after him, dodging kids, keeping the red flash in sight between backs and shoulders.

A tree root proved her undoing. She stubbed her toe hard and nearly fell. When she righted herself and dashed through the milling teenagers again, the red-painted jacket had disappeared. She stomped her foot in frustration. "Damn!"

Sharon joined her. "Find out anything?"

"Of course not. But I'm beginning to think this doesn't really have a lot to do with Proud Fox or the rockers against the straight kids or any of the other things we've been thinking it is."

"We need that kid."

Maggie licked her lips, a tremor of foreboding in her belly. "Yes, we do."

She got home a little later than usual to find Joel's truck parked in front of the house. He met her at the door to his apartment. "Go wash up," he said with a grin. "Dinner will be ready in ten minutes."

"You cooked?"

He lifted his chin proudly. "I'm not completely helpless."

Maggie snickered. "You burn *water*, Joel Summer."

"A man can learn a thing or two from a woman."

"True." She grinned. "I'll be right there."

After she'd changed into a pair of shorts and a softly woven cotton sweater, she returned to Joel's apartment. As always, the bookish clutter on his coffee table and couch made her smile, and she automatically began to straighten things, shifting papers into neat piles and stacking the books into a semblance of order.

Joel joined her. "I found some great stuff today," he said, looping his arms around her shoulders to nuzzle her neck.

At the delicious sensation, Maggie sagged against his strength, her hands going lax as she let her head loll back on his shoulder. "Really?" she asked lazily.

His broad palm slipped under her blouse and moved in circles over her belly. Against her ear, the smile obvious in his voice, he replied, "Really."

The familiar spiral of desire coiled up her legs as his hand roved more freely, brushing her breasts. "Joel," she said on a sigh, "how long do you think it will take us to get tired of this?"

"I can't speak for you," he said between nibbles on her neck, "but I doubt I ever will." With a playful slap to her bottom, he pulled away. "But right now, you have to come have your supper. I've been slaving over a hot stove."

"Not a microwave?" Maggie said, trailing him into the kitchen. The scent of grilled onions filled the air, mixed with something she couldn't quite pinpoint. On the table, set for two, were two bottles of beer next to tall, thin pilsner glasses. "Goodness," Maggie commented. "A glass and everything."

Joel flashed her a grin as he bent to open the oven, from which he withdrew two huge ceramic bowls. Inside, bubbling and lightly browned, she saw white cheese and a triangle of toast. He placed them on the table with a flourish, dimpling proudly.

"French onion soup?" Maggie said, delighted. "Did you make it from scratch?"

"Well, I had to buy some consommé, but I did the rest." He grinned again, blue eyes dancing. "Eat."

Touched and impressed, Maggie did as she was told. It was excellent—fragrant, well balanced and filling. The cold beer, poured alluringly into the elegant glasses, was the finishing touch. "My grandmother used to have some glasses like this," she said, "but we never drank beer from them. Only iced tea."

"A waste. I found these at an antique store this afternoon. Which reminds me..." He stood up, cocking an eyebrow before heading for the living room.

He returned with a cylindrical package tied with string. Maggie looked at him. "What is it?"

"Open it and see, silly."

When she'd torn away the green tissue paper, she laughed. It was a Barbie doll, vintage 1968, complete with psychedelic dress. "Oh, Joel! I had a doll exactly like this once."

"Great, isn't it?"

"It's wonderful." Impulsively, she hugged him. "Thank you."

He kissed her. "I love to bring you presents—you're always so delighted. Didn't people bring you things when you were a child?"

Shyly, Maggie shook her head. "Not really. My dad was a real stickler for the budget, and there wasn't a lot for extras." She clasped the doll to her chest. "Galen surprised me sometimes, but he left home when I was twelve." She looked at Joel. "Did people bring you lots of unexpected treats?"

His eyes danced. "Everybody did. Grandparents, parents, uncles, aunts—even my sisters. I had so much junk the guys always wanted to come over to my house and play."

"I'm glad," Maggie said. "You deserve to be spoiled."

The alarming soberness wiped his face clean of any other expression for an instant. "Come here," he said.

Maggie rose and settled on his lap. He nestled his head upon her breasts, enfolding her completely, and there was a strange intensity to his voice when he spoke again. "No surprise was ever as good as you are."

Maggie lifted a hand to his precious jaw, resting her cheek against his cool hair. A swell of love greater than anything she had ever known welled up inside of her. "I love you, Joel."

His kiss was nearly brutal as he stood, sweeping her up into his arms. He carried her into the living room and deposited her on the couch. There, he stripped away their clothes and took her in a fierce joining. The act was devoid of artificial coyness or even play—it was pure, elemental and devastating.

He awoke in the heavy stillness of early-morning dark, gasping for breath. In panic, he rolled out of bed, confused at his surroundings and intent only on getting air into his lungs. Pure terror filled his chest as he struggled, stumbling toward an open window. When he bent into its opening, the cool night splashed his face with a dose of reality, and he found the release to the attack. Here, there was a sky—he could see it, smell it, feel it.

In the aftermath of the panic, despair washed through him, a black hopelessness he'd grown to recognize. Through his mind flashed a picture of Nina, white and bloody and horrified. Her ugly screams, shrewish and shrill, echoed in his memory.

As if no time had passed, his stomach called up the last bit of the picture—his own cold realization that life would not ever be the same again.

Behind him, a hand reached out to touch his shoulder, and Joel started violently, whirling as if to strike. Seeing Maggie, hair tousled, eyes wide with fear, he let out a hard sigh and pulled her roughly into his arms. "I'm sorry," he breathed.

Maggie felt the trembling in his arms and soothed him with long strokes of her hands over his back. For a long, silent time, she stood with him by the open window, unmindful of the cold.

The foreboding she'd been feeling doubled, making a thick lump in her stomach. Beneath the teasing and the love, Joel harbored a closet full of demons. "The sky!" he'd called in his sleep, before bolting from the bed like a man pursued. In the simple words had been a longing of terrible vibrance. Maggie cradled him next to her, soothing, but her heart beat with fear.

She'd thought she could ignore whatever troubled him about his past. Now she saw that she could not. The pain needed the healing lance of confession.

That knowledge dogged her, manifesting itself in a tight lump that wouldn't leave.

She spent the morning on the phone, calling the numbers of parents culled from various lists on file at high schools around the city, to warn of the dangers involved in the concert scheduled for the next evening. Even as she dialed digit after digit, her frustration and worry grew; the reaction of most of the parents she reached was lukewarm. As the afternoon progressed, she wondered if she'd overreacted.

"Am I losing it?" Maggie asked Sharon when she came back with coffee in foam cups.

"What do you mean?"

"No one I've talked to seems to think there's anything to worry about. Is this a case of the media pumping up an issue?"

Sharon gave her a wry grimace and settled on the edge of Maggie's desk to stir cream into her cup. "You think about this, sweetie." With one long finger, she poked out the important words in her sentences. "We've covered six or seven demonstrations in three months. A total of about thirty-five children—and assorted others—have been injured, three seriously. We have no line on this Cory kid and no idea who's behind the demonstrations. We've also got to look at the fact that there will be thousands of kids at the Proud Fox concert." She widened her dark eyes. "Me? I'm worried."

Maggie tossed down a pencil. "My grandmother can't find any churches that will claim to be involved—and she knows a lot of people."

"You know," Sharon said, "maybe the original assumption that it was a church group was wrong."

"What about all the Bible verses on the signs and all that?"

"I don't know. Just a thought."

"Not much we can do now."

A voice from the doorway interrupted the conversation. "I'm looking for—"

Maggie jumped up in joy at the sight of the lean, tall blond man in the doorway. His longish hair was tousled as if from wind, his nose sunburned. "Galen!" she shrieked, and threw herself into his waiting arms. "I'm so glad to see you."

"You look great, kid," he said, holding her at arm's length.

She frowned. "You don't. You look like you never eat."

"I haven't gained or lost a pound since I was twenty-three," he said with a grin.

"Maggie's been spending time with a redwood tree," Sharon interjected, holding out a hand. "How are you, Galen?"

Flashing his charming grin, Galen grasped her hand in both of his. "Great. Are you still my sister's protector?"

"No, that's *photographer*," Maggie said with a laugh. She squeezed her brother's hand and looked at Sharon. "What do you say we shelve everything and head on over to my house? We'll have some drinks and a good meal."

"Terrific."

Maggie sent the other two home first, then stopped at a fruit stand on her way, collecting the ingredients for a fresh fruit salad to round out the manicotti she'd made.

She pulled into the driveway to find Sharon and Galen companionably swinging on the porch. "You could have gone inside," Maggie said. "That's why I gave you the key."

"Go inside on a day like this?" Galen shook his head. "You've forgotten how hot Albuquerque is. The Springs is always so cool."

"Enjoy yourself, then." Maggie shifted the bag on her hip. "I just have a few things to do for dinner, then I'll join you."

Sharon stood up. "I'll help you."

"No, you sit and keep my brother company. Anybody want a beer or a soda?"

"Pop for me," Galen said.

"Same here," Sharon added.

"I'll come in and get them," Galen said, standing. "Save you a trip."

He followed her into the kitchen, where she dropped her bag on the table and headed for the fridge for the manicotti. "Help yourself. I just have to throw this in the oven and make the salad."

Galen's eyes widened. "My sister cooking manicotti?" he said incredulously. "This is serious."

She laughed. "I'm finding I don't mind cooking as much as I once did. It's actually very creative."

"I've never known you to do anything except use Hamburger Helper," he said, taking two colas.

"I'm not that bad. I've always cooked Mexican food."

"When forced," he returned with a good-natured snort. He kissed her cheek. "I'm happy for you, sis. I can't wait to meet this guy."

"You'll like him," Maggie said with assurance.

He laughed. "I promise to be good."

"Just don't throw out intellectual puzzles to test him—he'll love it and I'll end up looking stupid."

"Okay." He headed out of the kitchen, and Maggie turned her attention to the food and table. After a few minutes, Galen and Sharon returned.

"Let me help," Sharon insisted, picking up an orange. "I know you hate to peel these things."

"Not all of us have daggers on the ends of our fingers."

Sharon waved her bright red nails. "Be Prepared is my motto."

"Galen," Maggie said, slicing bananas, "you ought to call Samantha. She'd been dying to see you. I've had three phone calls this week to find out if you were here."

"I'd planned to go see her tomorrow, maybe take her to lunch. You want to go?"

"I can't. We have a big story to cover. You go ahead, though. She'll love having you to herself." She grinned. "I'd suggest you take Gram, but she'd be bristling with disapproval toward Paul the whole time."

"I stopped and saw her this afternoon."

"Good." She stripped another banana of its skin. "You can use the phone upstairs, if you like."

Galen nodded. "I'll do that right now."

As he dashed upstairs, Sharon asked, "How's Sam doing?"

"Other than languishing for David," Maggie said with a grin, "she's fine. Her dad's given her the run of the darkroom, and she's had a blast."

"We can use her this fall as an intern."

"I agree. But you'll have to be her boss. I'm not objective enough." The sound of a truck distracted Maggie. "There's Joel." Wiping her hands on a towel, she dashed toward the door. As adolescent as it made her feel, she was hungry for the sight of him. One of her favorite times of day was the moment when she stood at the door, watching him come up the walk to her.

And today was no different. His gray shirt highlighted the leaping blue of his eyes and the deep tan of his skin. Sun flashed on his dark hair. As he saw Maggie, his face broke into a teasing smile and he strode easily, the powerful muscles of thighs and shoulders and arms meshing visibly to move him forward. As always, Maggie felt a thrill of delighted surprise that this man, this beautiful man, was focusing that gentle smile upon her.

He leaped up the steps and met her in the doorway with a playful growl, gathering her up in a hug. He kissed her deeply. "Hi."

Maggie grinned up at him. "Hi."

The glitter in her eyes added an exclamation point to his day, Joel thought with a grin, and grabbed one more quick kiss to last him through dinner.

At the sound of footsteps on the stairs, Joel glanced up, thinking Samantha had come home—and froze. The ice-blue eyes bore into him, and through a roar of white noise, Joel heard Maggie say, "I want you to meet my brother, Galen."

She tugged his hand and Joel moved forward one step, feeling the floor of his world give way.

Chapter Eleven

Galen continued down the stairs, pausing at the foot. "You must be—" he lifted a finger "—Joel."

Joel took the offered hand. "Hi, Galen."

For a long, pregnant moment, their eyes met. Each took the other's measure without speaking. Maggie, standing alongside, felt a prickle of unease. Would they dislike each other? All at once, her stomach twisted, a sensation completely out of proportion to the situation.

The quiet measuring of the men suddenly broke into ordinary conversation, and Maggie blew out a sigh. "I've got beer in here, Joel, or some coffee if you prefer."

"Coffee would be great, thanks."

"Okay." She shoved her hands into her pockets, glad for something constructive to do to stop the silly fluttering. "Dinner will be ready shortly."

Although she tried to divine the odd atmosphere in her kitchen during the meal, Maggie couldn't decide what was wrong. Joel and Galen seemed to get along fine, swapping tales of work and life-styles. When they moved to the subject of the blues, they eagerly discussed the merits of various recordings of favorite songs.

Sharon and Maggie talked both with them and around them, listening and questioning and throwing in asides of their own. If a bystander had viewed the tableau through the windows, he would have seen a gathering of laughing friends over a meal of some merit.

But it was what she sensed below the surface that disturbed Maggie. Joel and Galen seemed on some level to be having a completely separate conversation, using shorthand and double meanings to give and receive information unrelated to the topic at hand.

Not only that, Joel held her hand or touched her thigh throughout the meal. He was a naturally affectionate man, one of his most endearing qualities as far as Maggie was concerned, but she felt a difference in his touch tonight. It reminded her of the way Samantha and David had constantly held hands the week before Sam's departure.

Since there was nothing wrong to which she could quite give a name, Maggie finally decided she really was getting paranoid.

Then, as she passed the bread, Sharon shot Maggie a quizzical glance. The food Maggie had eaten turned to a lump of clay in her stomach. She wasn't imagining it—something really was wrong.

After the plates had been cleared, the little group wandered into the living room. A breeze through the screen door blew the smoke from Galen's cigarette into eddies of pale blue, and Maggie watched them musingly. What now? she thought.

Next to Maggie, Joel fidgeted with a rubber band, twisting it between his thumb and forefinger, over and over. His voice broke the difficult pause building in the room. "What's the plan for the concert tomorrow night?" he asked.

"David is going to meet us at the gate, and we'll just play it by ear." The burning in Maggie's stomach intensified, and she felt Joel's fingers land on the back of her neck, where they massaged gently at the taut muscles there. She flashed him a grateful look over her shoulder—and caught the most acute expression of sorrow in his eyes that she'd yet seen. It disappeared almost immediately.

"What concert?" Galen asked.

"Proud Fox, but we're not going for pleasure. Sharon and I are going to cover it for the paper."

"It's been a mess everywhere they've gone this summer," Galen said, stubbing out his cigarette. "Wear some pointed boots in case you have to kick your way out," he said with a smile, then stood up. "Sharon, let's go scare up some fun, shall we?"

"Thought you'd never ask, buddy. These two make you lonely, don't they?"

Joel awakened the next morning to a chorus of bird song outside the open windows of his bedroom. Beside him, gilded with the diffused light of the morning sun, Maggie slept deeply, one long leg thrown over his knees. Her skin glowed like honeyed fruit, and her full, pouty mouth was barely parted to let breath pass. Pressed softly into his side and hip were the curves of breast and belly he'd grown to know so intimately the past few weeks.

The past few weeks. Stolen time, now gone. He gave his eyes their last feast, letting them wash from her temple to her toes. When his eyes had finished, he stretched out a hand and followed the length of her back all the way down her spine, gently. Her flesh was velvety and supple.

When she stirred sleepily, reaching for him even as she dreamed, he bent to taste the column of her throat and the peach-soft cheeks. With one hand, he cupped a breast for the last time and felt a piercing, bittersweet pleasure at the eager pearling of the tip against his palm. He let his hands span her rib cage and fondle her bottom, and when she opened for him in the sweet, sleepy morning, he took sanctuary once more. He moved slowly, as if all their time were not gone, moved slowly to remember each brush of her breath on his chin, each nearly inaudible whimper in her throat.

Afterward, he didn't move because he couldn't bear to leave her. Her eyes, fawn brown and clear, opened to him at last. "I love you, Joel Summer," she said.

"You're the best thing that ever happened to me, Maggie. You changed my life." He kissed her one last time. "Don't ever forget that."

The gravity in his face frightened her. When he pulled away, she asked quickly, "Where are you going?"

"To make us some coffee. You can have the shower first." His voice sounded utterly normal as he stepped into a pair of jeans, normal enough that Maggie gave him a lazy grin. In the dust-moted light filtering through his curtains, he looked like a television jeans commercial—his dark hair tousled, powerful chest naked and feet bare. As he slipped out of the room, she wondered with a smile why his bare white feet made him seem sexy. A barefoot man isn't going anywhere, she thought, and headed for the shower with a wry twist of her lips.

A few minutes later, wrapped in a big terry-cloth robe, Maggie met Joel in the bedroom. He'd carried up two steaming mugs of coffee, but there was no food to go along with it. Joel ate a lot, and morning bread was not something he ever missed. "Where's the food?"

He paused, his hand in a drawer. "I'm sorry." His attitude was distracted. "Are you hungry? I didn't think about it."

Maggie frowned, her elbows and knees suddenly going a little wobbly. "I'm not in any hurry," she said.

Taking her cup, she sat on the edge of the bed. "Joel, what's wrong?"

The dark head moved once, side to side, as if to shake away a bad dream. Maggie saw his chest rise with a deep, long breath. He looked at her. "There's no easy way to do this," he said, and swallowed.

"Do what? You're scaring me."

"I'm sorry." He took a shoe box out of the drawer. For one more moment, he paused, then carried it to Maggie and gave it to her.

"What's this?" she asked. The terrible foreboding that had been building in her belly now spilled into her veins, raced to her heart and sent it thudding like the cannons at an army base.

"Open it," he said grimly. His hands were curled into fists. As she let her fingers edge along the lid, he suddenly turned away, then back again. "Just do it," he said harshly.

"I don't want to," she said. "I don't want to know. I don't care about the past. If I don't know about it . . ." She trailed off, unsure of what she meant.

He stared at her, his face set. "Open it."

Maggie tore off the lid—and her breath left her. Inside were dozens and dozens of letters, letters addressed to Mitchell Gray, care of the Colorado penal system. In Maggie's hand.

For a long time, she stared at them, her mind echoing. Of course. Of course the dinner last night had been so strange—Galen had known Joel instantly, for they'd been in prison together. Of course she'd felt as if she'd known Joel—she'd been writing to him seven years. Of course the photos in his living room, those bare, lonely photos, had triggered recognition—they were just like the drawings Mitchell used to decorate his envelopes.

In a voice hard and distant, one she hardly recognized as her own, Maggie asked, "So what's your real name?"

"Mitchell Joel Gray," he said. "Summer is my mother's name."

"You deliberately changed it so that I wouldn't know who you were."

"Yes." He made no effort to deny it, and Maggie realized she had expected an explanation.

"Why?"

He drew a breath. "I wanted to see if we would like each other in person."

"That's not it," she said, looking at him for the first time. "You didn't trust me to take you at face value."

"You're right." His blue eyes were cold. "I thought it was the right thing to do."

"How is a lie the right thing? Ever?"

"Maggie, I could tell from your letters, even if we didn't allow anything personal, that you wouldn't be able to handle the knowledge of my background. You'd have been artificially polite and scared to death."

"How do you know? I don't even know. You didn't give me a chance."

A note of impatience crept into his voice. "Come on, Maggie, this is no time to try and fool ourselves. You wouldn't have given me the time of day."

She jumped up, trembling. "So, you cooked up this elaborate plan to sucker me in—moving in next door like a stranger!"

"That wasn't the plan. My last place had cockroaches the size of dragons. I had to find something new." He shook his head. "When I looked in the paper, this place was open. I just took it." His posture eased a bit, and he held out a hand of entreaty. "Maggie, I'm sorry."

At the sight of the flat, wide palm, Maggie felt a redoubled sense of betrayal. "Don't touch me." The words were hard and cold. He pulled back.

Maggie flipped through the letters. The one on top was the last one she'd written, not three weeks before. "How did you manage to keep up the masquerade after you got out?"

"A guard helped me. He was my friend."

A whirl of violent emotion swelled up within her. Overcome with a fury she'd never known she possessed, she hurled the box across the room. It hit the wall with a thud, and rectangles of white exploded out of it, scattering all over the floor.

Joel grabbed her hands. "Take it easy, Maggie."

She stared at him, the mass of her insides so confused and torn she could barely breathe. "What did you do?" she asked, an edge of despair in her voice. "Did you kill your wife?"

"No." His eyes flared with emotion, and his jaw went hard. "I killed her lover."

"Oh, my God," Maggie said, reeling away from him.

Passion, she thought, her mind flooded with memories of her childhood, her father slapping her mother in a fit of fury; Galen screaming as his hair was chopped away viciously; Maggie cringing before him as he raged, spittle dotting her face as he screamed. Now her imagination chimed in: she saw Joel discovering his wife with her lover, saw the huge body and power aimed with fury at a man and saw that man fall. "I can't do this," she choked out, backing away from him. "I can't."

She turned and fled the room.

Joel wanted to throw back his head and howl, to somehow release the pain she was causing him by leaving. Instead, he grabbed his keys and headed for the only solace he knew. His birds and the open sky.

At first, Maggie couldn't decide what to do. She paced around her bedroom restlessly, wishing that she could tear out her heart the way animals chewed off a leg caught in a trap.

For a time she considered going to her grandmother, who would provide a shoulder to cry on. The problem was, Maggie couldn't imagine allowing her emotions to flow in the manner that would be necessary to cry. If she began, she thought she would never stop. Confession might be good for the soul, but it wasn't Maggie's style. Just as she'd felt uncomfortable discussing her attraction to Joel with anyone, she couldn't discuss his betrayal.

Finally, tired of roaming her room, she headed for the newspaper and the job awaiting her there.

The day passed in a blur. She couldn't decide whether to be grateful or disappointed when she found that Sharon wasn't at the paper. A note she'd left for Maggie explained she was following up a lead on Cory she'd gotten from a cop at a bar the night before. Turning on the radio for company, Maggie threw herself into planning the traditional Fourth of July issue on books.

But as she typed reviews, Mitchell's sharp analysis of books haunted her. Or rather, Joel's.

A bubble of pain broke within her. Maggie closed her eyes. He'd created an entire persona for her benefit, led her down the proverbial garden path like an expert. And she'd followed willingly, blindly naive. With a sharp, bitter sense of betrayal, she remembered how she'd created the category of sincere men, just for him. The irony grated on her wounds.

At five, Galen appeared at the door of the newspaper office. "Hi," he said. "What's up?"

Maggie knew by the expression in his eyes that he pitied her, and the knowledge made her furious. "What are you doing here?" she asked sharply. "I thought you were going to spend the night in Denver."

"I had a feeling you might need me."

She met his eyes, nostrils flaring. "I don't need your damned pity, Galen."

"I meant you might want someone to go to the concert with you."

"It's a bit late to be playing protector, don't you think?"

He raised his eyebrows and sighed. "Maybe."

"How did you know he'd tell me?"

"Because I know him."

"Do you know that he's a murderer?"

"Is that what he told you?" Galen frowned.

"He didn't go to prison for murder?"

"Yes." Galen straightened, seeming to come to a decision. He pursed his lips and took a step closer to his sister. "Look, I know you're hurting, but don't write him off yet, okay, kid?"

Maggie shook him off. "I already told you—you're too late."

Sharon arrived then, breathless and disheveled. "Maggie! I got everything."

"What?" Maggie leaped at the distraction. She hurried around the desk. "Tell me."

"The kid's name is Cory Silva. He's fifteen and until a year ago, racked up a bunch of charges in petty arenas—vandalism, car burglaries, that kind of thing. He's been in foster homes several times because his father is suspected of beating him, but he always goes home within a few months."

Maggie glanced at Galen, whose mouth thinned to a hard line. "Go on," she said to Sharon.

"He used to spend every waking moment with a brother who was a year older. Two years ago, at a Proud Fox concert in Denver, the brother was stabbed by a gang outside the arena and died."

"So," Maggie filled in, "he's on a vendetta."

"Right." Sharon flipped through some papers. "The cop didn't have a picture, but he gave me a good description. Cory has a long, thin scar on his face, from his mouth to his eye." She gave them a sober look. "Got it from his dad when he was four years old—nobody knows how."

A rush of excitement energized Maggie. "I know who he is," she exclaimed, grabbing her jacket. "I spoke to him one afternoon with Samantha, downtown. If we can find him in the crowd, maybe we can prevent any trouble."

"I'm going with you," Galen said firmly.

Maggie flashed him a hard look. "Do whatever you want."

He grabbed her arm as she began to turn away. "Don't blame me for your pain, Maggie." His face was grave. "You're all I've got."

The words reached past the wall she'd been hiding behind all day, and a quick rush of tears flooded her eyes—the first tears. "I won't," she said quickly, then hurried out of the offices behind Sharon, away from any reminder of Joel and his betrayal. If she worked hard, ignored the upheaval in her life, maybe it would all just go away.

That theory seemed to hold as the trio, joined by David at the entrance to the grounds, searched the concert area for any sign of Cory. There was an atmosphere of tense excitement infecting the air, and thousands of milling teenagers filled the grounds, their blankets spread on the grass under the sky.

Just outside the main gates, a small cluster of the familiar, neatly dressed teens marched in a solemn circle, carrying their signs and singing a hymn. Their number was small, Maggie thought, and they seemed to be having no impact at all on the eager crowd gathered to see the band.

Her lips formed a grim line. The night before the tickets had gone on sale, there had been no hint of trouble, either, she thought. Not until one rocker had suddenly started hitting the other kids. . . .

Realization struck her. "Cory isn't going to be with these kids," she said with certainty. "Look for a black leather jacket with a red pentagram on the back. He'll have long hair." As they split up to comb through the crowd, Maggie's stomach burned. All the pieces of the long puzzle aligned themselves—and the full picture chilled her. The reason she'd been unable to find any adults responsible for the protests was because there were no adults involved. Cory Silva, with the charisma of a teenage evangelist, had stirred up an incredible amount of trouble.

The discordant notes of the warm-up band's music and the general cacophony began to grate on her nerves, giving her a headache. After carefully scanning the portion of the crowd she'd agreed to search, she returned to the meeting spot. First Galen, then Sharon and David met her. "No luck," Galen said for all of them.

Maggie bit her lip. The sun had disappeared behind the craggy tips of the mountains, and a gray dusk spread over the field. "It's going to be harder and harder to find him," she said, her eyes flowing over the field and the less-favored seats above. "Maybe we ought to check the stands."

"What about calling his father?" Sharon suggested.

Maggie and Galen exchanged a glance. "No."

David looked impatient. As much as he wanted to participate in the drama of the search for Cory, Proud Fox would be on in a few minutes, and he'd been looking forward to the concert for weeks. Maggie smiled at him. "I think we can handle it from here, David. Thanks for your help. And be careful, okay?"

He lifted a hand. "No problem."

The opening band finished with a jangling crash of guitars. They departed the stage. "At least that's a relief," Maggie said with a sigh.

"I'll go check the stands," Galen said. "Don't go anywhere."

Maggie glared at him. "We're big girls, now, Galen."

"I just want to find you when I'm through," he answered evenly.

As he melted into the bodies, Sharon touched Maggie's arm. "Are you all right?"

Maggie considered a lie, but her heart wouldn't let her do it. "No," she said, and swallowed hard. She trained her eyes on the stage lights. "I found out that Joel is Mitchell." With a bitter laugh, she added, "Or Mitchell is Joel, however you want to look at it."

Sharon didn't answer immediately. "I thought so," she said.

"Well, thank you for sharing your insight," Maggie said sharply.

"Come on, Maggie. If I guessed, you had to have guessed yourself. You just didn't admit it."

"That isn't true," Maggie retorted. "I really didn't know, or I wouldn't have allowed the relationship to progress."

The volume of the crowd steadily rose. In the bleachers, the sound of stomping feet rocked the stands with steady thundering, and whistles and chants added to the noise. For one instant, Maggie thought of the day with Joel in Manitou, the first time he'd kissed her. For that moment, her world had seemed this alive, this vibrant.

With the memory came a clutch of excruciating pain to her stomach, and Maggie pressed her hands to it. Next to her, Sharon said, "Maybe you can work it out."

Maggie let go of a short near laugh. "Not a chance." she said. "This just proves my theory that you absolutely can't trust a man. Not any man."

"Your brother is a man."

Raising her eyes to Sharon's face, Maggie said slowly, "I know."

Chapter Twelve

As darkness fell, Joel knew what he had to do. Remembering his promise to move if anything happened to ruin the friendship between himself and Maggie, he went back to his apartment. He wandered through the spacious home, admiring the carved metal doorknobs and long windows, the bookshelves and the sunny kitchen.

Then, with a sense of resignation, he plunged into the work of moving himself out. He cleaned the recycling room, bagging cans and paper and plastic into neat bundles; swept and mopped the floors; boxed his record albums and tapes. A friend at the raptor center had agreed to store a few things for him. The rest he would take with him. There wasn't, after all, much of an accumulation.

Except his books. These he packed carefully into boxes and loaded into the cab of his truck. His books went with him. They had been the only constants of his life.

At last, he went upstairs. His bedroom was untouched since the morning's confession, and the sight of the letters, scattered like forgotten children on the floor, pained him. He picked them up carefully, shuffling them back into a neat, huge stack that contained all he had left of Maggie. These letters had shown him her resilience and strength, her humor and honor. They had been his beacon of light through the dark years, the one reason he could see in addition to his birds to continue to keep himself alive. Her thoughts and ruminations had given his mind and soul the fuel they needed to keep growing in an environment designed to thwart.

Even though he had lost her, there was no regret, not for himself. He had gambled all he had, given her all that he was, all that he had hopes of being. Even his lie had been perpetuated to protect her. A man could do no more. The past was not his to change.

As he gathered the letters to himself, smelling the scent of the potpourris he now knew she used in her bedroom, he had a brief, searing instant of sorrow. Maggie had truly given him his freedom—freedom to love again, freedom to laugh again. His most fervent hope had been to return that favor, to free her of the betrayals of her past.

Instead, he'd given her one more. Unlike Moses, she'd required more than shelter and nourishment. In that one kernel of truth, he found his regret. Maggie deserved so much more, and he'd been unable to deliver.

Galen had no luck in the stands. "I think I'll find him in the front of the crowd."

"What makes you say that?"

He frowned. "If I wanted to start a riot, that's where I'd go. The crowd is thickest there, rowdiest. Stands to reason."

"All right." Maggie rubbed a throbbing temple. "Let's go."

"Why don't you stay here? I'll go check it out."

"Forget it Galen. I'm a newspaper publisher, remember? I'm aware of the risks."

He hesitated, then shrugged. "Fine. Let's do it before the band comes on."

Unfortunately, the press of the crowd was resistant to allowing even one more body to pass through its mass, and before the trio had inched even halfway toward the front, Proud Fox ran onstage.

The crowd had been waiting months for this moment, and they exploded with their enthusiasm, screaming, jumping, shouting, whistling and clapping. Wedged into the midst of them, Maggie was jostled and shoved. Her eardrums felt as if they would burst under the pressure of noise. When the band slammed into their first song, a decibel level Maggie would have sworn caused deafness was trebled. Every cell of her brain sizzled with the initial powerful rocket of sound.

But as she'd told Galen, she was aware of the risks. The thought of the possible mayhem that could result if a riot broke out in this madhouse spurred her on. Ignoring the glares flung at her, she squeezed through one row of teens after another, shouldering and elbowing and dipping to get through. After what seemed like an endless time, she found herself three rows from front and center. Looking up to regain her bearings, her gaze froze on a black jacket painted with a red pentagram, an impossible squeeze to her right, on the fringes of the crowd.

The boy in the jacket flipped long hair away from his face, and Maggie noted the wig was slightly askew. His face was in profile. In the bright lights from the stage, she could see the twist of his lips and the fine scar running from his eye through his cheek. As she watched, Cory reached into his pockets and withdrew a handful of round, dark balls.

She frowned, pushing past two more people, then a third, trying to see what he was doing. A match flared in his hand, an unremarkable event in the crowd of smokers.

Then Maggie saw him touch the match to the fuses on the balls, lighting several at once before tossing them like volleyballs into the crowd. In shock, Maggie saw one sail toward her, the fuse sparkling orange against the night sky.

Without conscious thought, feeling as if she were moving in slow motion, she shoved at the people in front of her, violently moving through the resistant stream toward the spot she thought the firecracker would land. It was a cherry bomb, probably, not designed to do more than cause a lot of noise, but if it exploded in someone's face—

It landed before Maggie could reach the spot, the noise of the explosion muffled in the electric guitar pouring from the speakers. But around the landing spot, kids screamed and jumped back, shoving those behind and in front of them, which in turn, caused those people to shove and push back. As she watched, the ripple of irritated pushing grew, like the radiating circles expanding from a rock thrown into a pond. Around her, she heard the other cherry bombs go off with sharp reports like gunfire, saw the same principle in action.

An elbow caught her chin with dizzying force, making her teeth clack together with jarring noise. When Maggie shook off the stunning blow to look around, Cory was gone.

No, not gone, she saw—deeper in the crowd. He'd taken advantage of the milling confusion caused by his cherry bombs to fuse himself with the shifting bodies. The move had brought him only a few feet from Maggie.

With her goal in sight, she felt a surge of adrenaline give power to her body. She pushed through the last obstacles like a needle through cloth, simply and directly.

She grabbed the leather-jacketed arm and ripped off his wig. "Don't do it!" she shouted in his ear. Twisting his arm behind his back with more strength than she knew she had, Maggie pushed him ahead of her, out of the crowd. "I know who you are!"

He fought her, not much at first, but more and more as they neared the outer rim of people. He kicked her in the shin hard. With the pain came a blinding red anger, a renewal of the same fury she'd felt upon learning of Joel's betrayal. Adrenaline-spurred power gave her arms twice as much strength as they ordinarily had, and she shoved Cory with all her might toward a security guard.

Cory broke free, struggling the last few feet to the corridor of space near the fence. Maggie took off after him, determined she would not lose him this time, not if it killed her. He darted toward the gates leading to the bleachers, glancing once over his shoulder at Maggie, following close behind. He seemed to hesitate, then bolted up the stairs at a pace only a young, healthy boy could meet.

As Maggie took the stairs, her breath tore raggedly in and out of her chest. Each lungful of air seemed to have gained sharp edges, and her throat hurt. Adrenaline had helped her begin—now stubbornness would not let her give in.

He ran clear to the top of the bleachers and turned desperately to the right, looking for an out. Maggie forced rubbery legs up the last few stairs. She cornered him at the top level of the arena, where a wind cut through the opening to their left. Bleachers descended in stairs for hundreds of feet in the other direction—bleachers filled with fans.

As Maggie neared him, he charged her with a yell. She stood firm, absorbing the tackle with a cocked shoulder, the way she had as a child with Galen, and effectively blocked him. They both fell to their knees, and Maggie reached her arms around the boy's torso, pinning him against her.

His body went limp. "Oh, God," he cried. "Oh, God." He covered his face with his hands.

Not entirely certain this wasn't another ploy to escape, Maggie released her hold a fraction. He sagged further under the weight of the sobs shaking his shoulders, and Maggie released him entirely, braced to snag him again if he ran.

He didn't. He collapsed completely on the concrete floor, weeping uncontrollably. "I just wanted to make it up to him," he cried, taking Maggie's hand. "He was all I had!"

Maggie thought of Galen. "I understand, Cory. More than you'll ever know." She took his hand. "But this wasn't right. You need help."

"No!" His face paled, the scar that twisted his mouth standing out in relief. "God, please don't tell my father. He'll kill me."

Maggie fought to control her voice. "You have my personal guarantee that you won't ever have to go home to him again."

Cory moved away, panic clear in his eyes. "They always say that and they always send me back. You just can't know...!"

"Listen to me!" she shouted. "My father was a brutal, vicious man, just like yours. I do know what I'm talking about."

He looked at her.

"My brother is an expert on both the beatings and the ways the state can protect you. He's here, at the concert, and he can get you the help and the shelter that you need." She faced him squarely, her voice hard. "I'll take you to him, right now. But I swear, if you pull anything, I'll press charges for this cut on my eye, for the vandalism to my house, and I'll see you in court for the riot at the ticket outlet." She let the words sink in for a moment. "What's it going to be?"

Cory stood, his posture exhausted. "I'll go see your brother."

"Good for you." She cocked an eyebrow. "Don't mind if I hold your arm, do you? My legs are a little shaky after that run."

It was nearly an hour before they found Galen, waiting near the gates to the parking lot. In all that time, Cory docilely followed her instructions. It disturbed her in a way—the confrontation seemed to have taken everything he had. In spite of all the violence he'd perpetuated, she found herself feeling a deep sympathy for the boy. She honestly hoped he would find the help he needed, that it wasn't too late to educate him to healthier ways of venting emotion.

She sketched the situation to Galen quickly. He didn't need much information, only the appeal for help. As she'd known he would, Galen took charge immediately. "You can go home now, Maggie," he said, touching her cheek. "You need some rest."

Joel's truck was gone and his apartment windows were dark when Maggie drove up in front of the building. She was aware only of a sense of relief as she dragged herself up the steps.

Letting herself inside her own apartment, she collapsed on the couch in the darkness. For a long time, she just sat there, feeling the emptiness of the rooms reflected in her heart. It was a loneliness as bereft of hope as any she'd ever experienced, even worse than the day Galen had run away from home.

That thought gave rise to another. In her mind's eye, Maggie saw herself manhandling Cory Silva on the field. She felt a fleeting wisp of the living anger that had spurred her and shook her head in bewilderment.

Never in her life had she allowed any kind of anger to break her composure. Even when Samantha, as exasperating and exhausting as all children are, had pushed Maggie to the limit, she hadn't given in to the furious, all-consuming rage that had engulfed her tonight.

Its appearance terrified her. In those moments, she knew with cold certainty that if it had been necessary to knock Cory down to stop him, she would have done it. She'd have knocked him senseless if the need had arisen.

How could her control, the control developed over a lifetime, have snapped so completely?

She shivered, thinking of the morning's revelations. As the full scope of Joel's betrayal had become clear to her, she'd experienced another emotion alien to her—hatred. For a long violence of seconds, she'd hated Joel Summer with every infinitesimal piece of herself. It made her feel ill now to think of it.

Wrapping her arms around her legs, she tried to halt the trembling of her limbs. Anger and hate had both come from love. The passionate, overwhelming love she'd allowed herself to feel for Joel.

But it hadn't been love that had seduced her, in the end. Joy had done that. It had been joy that had shimmered between them as they'd made love, an emotion as clear and perfect as the first morning light. Its perfection had lulled her into believing it would be safe.

Unfortunately it was impossible to open the door to just one emotion. By removing the blocks to joy, she'd also let anger and sorrow and despair into her life. She should have known that, should have already learned this lesson.

Before she could cry, Maggie stood up. She would close the door to all of them again. Love would become again a tenderness she felt toward Samantha and Galen, anger nothing more than mild irritation. She would allow no intrusion of Joel Summer into her thoughts until she felt nothing, not hate or sorrow or love. Until his memory brought only a mild, distant regret, she couldn't allow him any space in her mind.

The trick, she thought wearily, heading upstairs to her own bed, a bed she'd not slept in for weeks, was finding out how to keep herself from thinking of him.

He made it easier, as it turned out. Sunday morning, it was apparent that he was gone. Not just out for the day, but packed up and gone. When Maggie realized it, she felt a pang for the cats, Moses and Buddy. She would miss them.

When Galen came downstairs for breakfast, he said, "It looks like Mitchell moved."

The sound of his real name sent a sharp, hot sword through her middle, and Maggie had to breathe deeply against it for a moment. "I know," she finally answered, focusing her attention on the counter she was wiping.

"That's odd," Galen commented as he took a seat at the table.

Maggie shook her head. "No, he promised he would move if we found we couldn't get along." In spite of everything, it was no surprise to find that he'd kept that promise.

"Do you want to talk about this, Maggie?"

"No," she said flatly.

He scanned her face with a worried frown. "All right," he said finally. "It's your little red wagon." He stood up. "But I can't sit around here and watch you brood. Let's do something."

"What?"

"I don't know. We'll think of something."

"You go ahead," she said. "I don't really feel like doing anything."

"I'll stay, then. I came here to be with you."

"No sense in your suffering with my bad mood."

He settled back in his chair stubbornly. "All the same..."

"Have it your way," she said. "What happened with Cory last night?"

"About time you got around to asking."

She shrugged listlessly.

"He's going to be evaluated and moved accordingly. By the time I got him to the shelter last night, he was blubbering like a baby, sobbing about that brother of his. It's pretty clear he's not stable, that he hasn't grieved."

"Is there any hope for him, do you think?"

"Oh, yeah," Galen said with a grin. "There's always hope. If I didn't believe that, I wouldn't be in the line of work I am."

She smiled halfheartedly.

"Maggie." His voice was stern.

"Don't, Galen," she said in a weary voice. "Please."

He reached out and took her hand. "Do you remember what you used to do when Dad went crazy?"

She frowned, wondering what this had to do with anything. "Not really." With a droll twist to her lips, she added, "I frankly avoid thinking about him at all."

Galen licked his lips. "You used to hide under the stairs. It was full of spiders, but you braved your greatest terror rather than face Dad." He stroked her fingers gently. "I would find you under there, shivering, with your hands around your knees, pale as a ghost.''

The memory flashed on the screen of her mind, vivid and intense. A rush of hot tears filled her eyes, and she snatched her hand from her brother's to cover the trembling of her lips. "Damn you, Galen," she whispered. "You're the only one who can do this to me."

"You're hiding now like you did then," he said quietly. "I'm not going to tell you what to do, one way or the other, but you have to deal with it."

The tears, irrepressible now, slid over her face. "I don't know how."

"Find a way," he said, standing and reaching out for her.

Maggie collapsed in his arms, weeping. He held her while she cried, the way he had when she was seven. She let her mind go where it would as the cleansing tears flowed through her. She saw herself with Joel in the high mountain meadow, laughing with giddy pleasure as the kite tugged on the string between her fingers. She saw his great head bending to taste reverently of her breasts and saw his eyes, trained with familiarity on the sky. "God, Galen," she said with a broken voice, "I really fell for him."

"I know you did." His hand smoothed her hair gently, calming her.

The words seemed to provide a cork on her emotions, and wiping at her eyes, Maggie pulled away. Galen said nothing as she walked to the sink to splash cold water on her hot eyes, then dried them. Finally, she turned. "Did he do it?"

Galen sighed, lifting his heavy blond eyebrows ruefully. "I wish I could say no. The truth is, he would never discuss it." He paused. "What do you think?"

Maggie shook her head slowly. "I don't know." She took a breath and blew a strand of hair away from her face. "That's not even really the issue, is it?"

"Maybe it is."

"He lied to me, Galen. Invented somebody. I feel now like I was the only participant in what I thought was something really good."

"What do you think you really would have done if he'd shown up at your door and introduced himself?"

"That's exactly the point," she cried. "He didn't trust me enough to give me the chance."

Galen nodded. "I see what you mean."

"Oh, please," Maggie protested with irritation, "don't play psychologist with me, counselor."

"Okay," he said, straightening. "I'll talk like your brother. That man is crazy in love with you. He lied. I understand why that upsets you. I can also see, knowing you, why he did it." He pursed his lips in consideration, "About his killing his wife's lover—I don't think it matters. He's done his time and he's not a crazed killer."

"Nobody ever thought Ted Bundy was a killer, either."

"Maggie, I've been on the inside, and believe me, I'm glad they built prisons. Mitchell—or Joel—didn't belong there from the first minute he walked through the gates.''

Maggie looked at her brother. If only she could see it so clearly, without the weight of her obligations and the burden of the past. She shook her head. ''If it were just me, I might take the chance. But not as long as I've got Samantha.''

He shrugged. ''You do whatever you think you have to. I do think you ought to know one more thing.''

''What?''

''Even in prison, he never allowed his dignity to be insulted. If you decide you want him, you're going to have to make the first move. He never will.''

Maggie looked at her hands. If that was the case, it was over.

She wondered why it felt so unfinished.

Chapter Thirteen

On Thursday, just after Anna had shown up with double her usual amount of doughnuts, a pale gray car pulled up in front of the building. It was an older model Maggie didn't recognize, loaded with suitcases. "Must be the new tenants," she said from the window. Her voice was calm, but underneath, she felt the never-distant needle of sorrow. It was final, she thought. Joel was gone for good.

Galen glanced over her shoulder. "Put your glasses on, babe," he said, teasing.

Maggie squinted, a habit she'd found herself falling back on again recently. "Maybe it's time for contacts," she commented when even squinting wouldn't bring the figures climbing out of the car into focus. "Who is it?"

"One cute blonde, definitely too young," Galen said.

"What?" She hurried toward the door, and finally the blurry figure melded into one recognizable to her strained eyes. "Samantha!" she said as she ran out the door, the screen slamming hard behind her.

Sam dropped her bags to throw herself into her mother's arms. "Iii!" She squeezed Maggie's neck hard, rocking. "I've missed you."

"Oh, honey, I've missed you, too." She pulled back to view the array of suitcases. "What's going on? You aren't due home for weeks."

She grinned impishly. "Dad got a plummy assignment. I just happened to overhear him refusing it, and I talked him into letting me come home early."

"I'm glad," Maggie said, giving Sam one more quick hug. "Come on in. Gram's just brought a bunch of pastries."

David, who'd driven, hung close to the car. "I'll let you guys visit," he said. "Sam, I'll see you later, okay?"

"Oh, no you don't." She grabbed his arm firmly. "You come inside with the rest of us."

With a touching blush, he glanced at Maggie. "I've seen you," he said. "Your mom hasn't."

"She doesn't care," Sam insisted, and glanced at her mother. "Do you?"

Maggie laughed. The sound was a little rusty in her throat, but it qualified as the real thing. "Of course I don't. Come on, David."

On the way up the steps, Samantha looped her arm through Maggie's. "Guess what I got?"

"No telling." Paul often sent Samantha home with wildly expensive gifts.

"A black-and-white enlarger of my very own. Dad said I'm good enough that I need to start practicing all the time." The glitter in her eyes told Maggie that Sam knew the gift had been a balm to Paul's guilty conscience—and that she didn't mind in the least. "Do you think we might be able to rig up a darkroom someplace in the house?"

"I'm sure we can."

As they went inside, Samantha hugged and kissed the others, chattering about her trip and the things she'd done. Her presence, Maggie thought, was refreshing. Even her appearance was cheerful—bright blue shorts and crisp white blouse. Her hair was fastened in a blue-and-white clip shaped like a butterfly. As she talked, she moved and bounced and laughed. For the first time in a week, Maggie felt the stirrings of life within her.

"So, how's Joel?" Sam asked.

"He moved," Maggie said.

Galen jumped into the conversation quickly. "Why don't you get that fancy camera and show it off? We aren't all together like this very often."

"Okay." She headed for the car, but not before flashing her mother a quizzical glance.

Maggie shifted to place a hand on her brother's arm, giving it an unobtrusive squeeze of thanks. He patted her hand in solace, even as he laughed at some ribald joke Gram made.

That night, in spite of the whirl of activities Sam's return home had inspired, Maggie couldn't sleep. Long after the last creaks and whispers of the house had settled behind Galen and Samantha, Maggie stared into the darkness. After twenty minutes of that, getting nowhere, she crept downstairs for potato chips and beer, then watched two episodes of *Star Trek*.

None of it helped. Her mind restlessly whispered with memories and visions she couldn't quell, no matter how hard she tried.

She missed him—or rather, *them*. Mitchell, whose letters had always been a private, personal pleasure, and Joel, who had shown her the beauties of the spirit and flesh. Mind, body and soul, she thought. Between them, they'd satisfied the entire triad.

Jumping up, she strode to the tiny office off her bedroom and yanked open a desk drawer. There, neatly filed according to postmark, was every letter Mitchell had ever written. The first day of his betrayal, she'd considered burning them in a melodramatic gesture of fury. Now she was glad her saner self had won out.

Making a basket out of her nightgown, she grabbed chunks of letters until the drawer was empty, then carried them to her bed. There, she dumped them unceremoniously onto the quilt, scattering seven years of her life.

The envelopes were all decorated with painstaking beauty. There were animals and seascapes and trees, boulders and tiny flowers. As she examined them, she noticed two things she'd never seen before. Always the sky was deep and blue, like the sky over the Rockies on a clear spring day. And always, swooping through the heavens, was a bird.

Suddenly, she remembered the nightmare that had sent Joel, sweating, to the window for air. Just before he'd been torn from sleep, he'd cried out for the sky.

The memory pricked her heart. For the first time, she understood how difficult prison had been for him, how he'd mourned the loss of the open sky.

On impulse, she sifted through the dozens and dozens of letters to find the very first one he'd written to her. Slipping it out, she began to read his well-formed thoughts in the bold, slanting hand. This was the letter outlining the restrictions he needed her to agree to before they could write to each other. Maggie had forgotten how firm he'd been about it: no personal information at all. He didn't want to know how old she was or whether she was married or if she had children. All he needed was a place to air his thoughts, someone to share those musings with.

The letter transported her back to the days of loneliness she'd experienced before her divorce from Paul. Mitchell's letters had seemed a godsend at the time. He'd made her laugh with dry comments about the political scene, had made her think with sharp insights about the world. Each time the mailman had delivered one of his colorful envelopes, Maggie's spirits, no matter how low, had lifted.

She'd forgotten that, how precious and tenuous the relationship between them had been in the beginning. Only time had solidified their need for the other's thoughts.

With a pensive sigh, she refolded the letter, choosing another at random. When she finished it, she picked up another, then another and another, reading until dawn broke the night with gold fingers.

When at last she returned the letters to their drawer, her eyes burned with the reading, but one thing was clear. Before Joel Summer had ever appeared in her life, she had loved Mitchell Gray. No other person on earth had ever known her mind as intimately as he had.

Where that knowledge left her was less clear. In a way, she felt even angrier, for Joel had stolen Mitchell away, and Mitchell had been the most solid cornerstone in her life. The pen pal who didn't judge, always listened to and honored her opinions in a way that no one else had in Maggie's entire life.

Somehow, she realized as she made a pot of morning coffee for the house that had not yet risen, she needed to synthesize the two parts of the man she loved. Only then could she make peace with his past.

It was still so hard to imagine either side of him being capable of murder. Everything about him spoke of his respect and love of life in all its forms.

With a start of surprise, she realized she didn't think he had done it. Could it have been Nina who'd actually killed the man?

Getting a little desperate, aren't you? she asked herself with irritation. And maybe she was. She simply couldn't imagine living her life without him—whichever *him* he turned out to be.

Nor could she see herself agreeing to love, honor and cherish a man who had been convicted of murder. What she needed, to make sense of all of it, was the critical, missing information. She needed to know what had happened.

It took some research, since Maggie didn't know exact dates, just general time periods. In the library of the daily newspaper, she looked up first the wedding announcement of Mitchell and Nina Gray. It was simple and to the point, giving Maggie the information she needed: Nina's maiden name was Hunt.

Next, she looked up the murder trial and worked backward to find the original police report, which simply stated that Mitchell had been taken into custody after a forty-year-old auto salesman had been killed under suspicious circumstances.

The trial reports held little of interest. By the time it had taken place, the city had grown large enough and violent enough that one murder trial was not much to write about. There was, however, one photograph that Maggie found electrifying.

Joel, his hair shorn into a severe cut, stood just outside the courtroom in a well-cut suit. His eyes,

electrically blue even in a black-and-white photograph, were trained on the haughty woman walking
toward him. Her heavy, dark hair swung in a bell
around her shoulders. Maggie's eyes narrowed at the
expressions of the two principals, frozen for all time
in the photograph. On Nina's face was a definite smirk
of satisfaction.

Joel's face showed not the hatred Maggie would
have expected, but an unmistakable mask of sorrow.
Whether it was for the loss of this love or the loss of
his freedom, Maggie had no way of knowing. She did
know the expression pierced her.

She closed the book of newspapers, fingering the
slip of paper with Nina's name. The reason she'd come
to the paper this morning was to learn Nina's last
name, with the vague aim of confronting her about the
night of the murder. There was something odd about
it, as nigglingly out of kilter as the demonstrations
against Proud Fox had been.

In the end, she went to the courthouse and looked
up the transcripts of the trial. It took hours to sort
through the judgments and legalese, but Maggie finally found what she was looking for: Testimony from
both Joel and Nina.

It was painful, she discovered, for she heard every
word of Joel's terse account in his rich, bass voice. A
part of her ached for him, her gentle lover, in his moment of darkness, and she was acutely angry at Nina,
who should have supported her husband in his crisis.

Instead, Nina's testimony seemed designed to in-
criminate Joel even further. As she read, Maggie saw

again the beautiful woman's expression in the news-paper photograph—meanly triumphant.

By the time Maggie finished, her eyes were weary with nearly twenty-four hours of reading, and her neck ached from bending over the transcripts. She headed home with a whirl of thoughts spinning in her mind.

Galen and Samantha were just about to sit down to dinner, and Maggie joined them, but she was dis-tracted throughout the meal. "I'm sorry, you two," she said, carrying her plate to the sink. "I know I'm a million miles away, but I've got to get some sleep."

"That's all right, Mom. We understand."

"Good," Maggie said vaguely, and drifted upstairs and to sleep.

Joel spoke softly to a tiny screech owl, newly ad-mitted and terrified. The bird's yellow eyes were wild with fear and pain, darting from Joel to the hunk of meat in front of him. Joel chuckled quietly. "Go on, little one," he coaxed. "It's not what you're used to, but I think you'll like it, anyway."

Out of the corner of his eye, he thought he saw a swath of honey-gold hair in the parking area. His heart squeezed and leaped simultaneously before he remembered that it wouldn't be Maggie.

He'd been half seeing her in his peripheral vision for the endless, endless days since that morning in his bedroom. Any long-legged woman, any head of honey hair, any woman with Maggie's firm, purposeful stride caught his eye, made his heart constrict until he could see that none of them was her.

A footstep in the gravel nearby made him look up, and for a second his heart stopped completely. This time, it really was Maggie.

She stood next to him, and Joel looked away. "If you had just trusted me, we could have avoided a lot of pain," she said quietly.

"I thought we've already been through this," he said, his voice reflecting his punctured hope.

"Not this part."

He looked at her. "What part, Maggie? The murder?"

Maggie took a long, slow breath, stealing herself against his incredible beauty. In one week, her mind had erased some of the perfection of that face, and seeing it in all its glory proved more difficult than she had anticipated. "It wasn't murder," she said finally. "The charge was manslaughter."

"Big difference, right?"

"I think there is." She shifted in the gravel. "Why don't you tell me about it."

He rose from his squatting position. His jaw was hard. "You obviously know enough. Why don't you tell me?"

This was a side of him she hadn't seen. No emotion showed on his face, no translucent light shone in his eyes. This was Mitchell facing her—Mitchell, who'd learned to survive in prison. "You thought he was killing her," she said.

He blew out a lungful of air, touching his chest in a vulnerable gesture. "Yeah." His eyes focused high on the horizon. "She called me at work, terrified. We were split up by then, but I went to her rescue the same way I always did." His fist clenched and lifted, fell impotently back to his side.

"When I got to her house, I heard her screaming. It scared the hell out of me. I ran up the steps and tore into the room—" He shook his head, licked his lips. "There was this ape in there, throwing her around like a rag doll. She had blood on her face and she was screaming, and something in me just broke." He swallowed. "I didn't mean to kill him, Maggie," he said. His voice was subdued.

"What did you do?"

"Look at me," he said, and now myriad emotions raced through his voice, which had risen in regret and remorse. He held up his hands in front of him, like a surgeon awaiting his sterile gloves. "My whole life I've been bigger than anyone around me, stronger than three guys put together. All the way through school, guys challenged me to fight so they could prove themselves. The coaches wanted me on the football team so I could mow down all the little guys playing quarterback and center." He raised his eyes. "My dad always said, 'Boy, you let them break on you. Don't ever hit 'em back.'" He shook his finger as he imitated his father.

Maggie thought then there might be something she should say. But she needed to hear it all and remained silent to listen.

After a moment, he said, "So I always let them break on me. I didn't play football and I didn't fight. I had no idea what my hands could do to a man." He paused. "I wish to God I'd never found out."

It was impossible to check her tears then. She loved him too much to avoid feeling his pain. But with that first emotion, all the others she'd been holding back were released, as well.

Hearing her sob, he looked up. "Maggie..." he began.

"No. You listen to me now. I'm hurt because you didn't trust me, not with your real self when you wrote to me and not with the other parts of yourself when you became Joel. Now I'm having a little trouble putting the two people together. I don't know who I'm talking to or who I love." Her voice broke and she furiously dashed away her tears.

"You and Galen keep talking about how necessary it was that you lie to me, that I wouldn't have accepted you if you had come to me as Mitchell." She straightened her shoulders. "Well, I have news for both of you—I would have welcomed Mitchell, because I already loved you. Now I don't know what to do."

He stepped forward, his hope blazing anew. She stepped back to ward him off. "I'm not ready yet, Joel—" she shook her head "—Mitchell. You see?" she cried. "I don't even know what to call you!"

She whirled to hide the tears that blinded her. With her back turned, she added, "The thing that makes it so terrible is that you and Galen are the only men I've ever trusted. And neither of you trusted me in return."

Before he could say another word, she bolted for the car. When she reached it, she burst into huge sobs, gripping the steering wheel. She had come here to sort things out with him and had botched it completely. Never in her life had she been so confused.

Chapter Fourteen

Galen left Sunday morning. Sunday afternoon, the new neighbors moved into the other half of the building, which never went unrented for long. It was a young married couple, a fact Maggie viewed with more than a little irony.

The letter came Monday morning, the only thing the postman delivered. Before she even lifted a hand to pull it out of the box, she knew who it was from by the deeply colored sky visible on the edges of the envelope. For an instant, she hesitated, then withdrew it.

At first glance, there was no difference in the drawing. A single hawk circled above her name and address, written in the familiar bold hand. As her trembling hands carried the slender envelope closer, she saw that Moses with his many toes graced one corner. Curled deeply in the hollow between his paws was the kitten Buddy. And on the left of her name stood Maggie in a meadow, her hands lifted around a ball of string that trailed below her name to attach itself to the flying bird—a kite.

Again, he'd quoted Longfellow on the bottom of the envelope. "Love is sunshine, hate is shadow, Life is checkered shade and sunshine, Rule by love, O Hiawatha!"

Her throat tight, she carried the letter inside and sank down onto the nearest seat. It was impossible to simply tear it open, her hands shook so terribly, and she had to wait for them to calm a bit.

Finally, she turned it over and slipped loose the glued flap to pull out a single sheet of paper.

Dear Maggie,
This is the last card I have to play. When I wrote you from prison, I couldn't afford the luxury of emotion. Now there are no such restrictions.

And I find I have no words to tell you how I feel. For days I've sought the perfect phrase—I've combed every poetry book I own, reread every passage in every love story that I know of. Nothing fits because you are unique.

So humbly, I draw.

Love, Joel.

Below, he'd sketched a radiant ball of light. Around

it curled broken prison bars. In the center of the light was Maggie's face.

Maggie found him on a hill with a prairie falcon she recognized as the one that had snagged a field mouse for Joel one sunny afternoon. Since he was unaware of her, she watched him for a long time, his letter pinched between her fingers in the pocket of her skirt.

Never had the perfect balance between size and grace been more carefully achieved. Never had colors been so beautifully arranged, from the bright, clear blue of his eyes to the palette of blacks and reds that made his hair.

It was no accident that he loved these birds, these fierce and beautiful birds of prey. Like the hawk he'd mourned with Maggie in their lilac-scented backyard, he had failed to thrive away from the sight of the open sky. And like all birds of prey, he killed only in defense of his own.

As she watched, he untied the jess on the falcon's leg and moved his arm to launch the bird into the azure sky. The falcon circled, higher and higher, testing the currents of wind. Joel lifted his face to watch it, and Maggie saw his throat work with emotion.

The bird beat its powerful wings, and with an amazing display of speed, flew away. Maggie followed its flight until it disappeared, then looked up to find Joel's eyes upon her.

She climbed the hill, unabashedly letting her tears flow hot over her face, tears of joy and release. In the knee-high yellow grass at the top of the hill, she stopped. "I was wrong to judge you so harshly," she said. "I don't care what your name is." She swallowed to give her throat room for words. "I love you."

With a quick sound of joy, he swept her into a rib-crushing hug. Against her neck, he breathed, "I missed you." He pressed his lips to her neck, her jaw, her eye, finding at last her mouth, which he claimed in joy.

Maggie met his passion eagerly, feeling the light burst once again within her. Pulling away a fraction of an inch, she said, "I can't believe I considered actually letting this go."

As if the thought pained him, Joel pressed her head into his shoulder. "I was so afraid that you would, that I would have lost you." His chest expanded with a breath, and he eased his hold to look at her. "I don't believe we've been properly introduced," he said.

"You don't have to do this," Maggie protested.

"My name is Mitchell Joel Gray. Everyone but my mother and the state of Colorado has always called me Joel."

She nodded. "Joel, then." She smiled. "Samantha is going to be thrilled. She's been mad that you moved and took the cats ever since she got home."

"She's back home?"

Maggie nodded.

"That means no more making love, then."

"No. I'm not going to pretend to be something I'm not. I'm in love with you, I'm grown, and sometimes sex is a part of a relationship like that."

He said nothing for a moment, measuring her. "It's also sometimes a part of marriage."

"Is that what you want?"

The dimples in his cheeks flashed deeply. "Well, I don't want to spend another seven years getting to know someone else," he joked. "Of course that's what I want," he said, suddenly sober.

"And children? More of them, I mean? Will you want to do that?"

"Do you want more children?"

The tears sprang to her eyes again. "Oh, yes, Joel. And I can't think of anything I'd like more than being your wife."

"You're sure you feel okay about my past?"

Maggie nodded. "I may still have some things to work through about that. It may not always be easy for you."

"As long as I'm with you, Maggie, I really don't care."

She laced her fingers with his as they started down the hill. "We'll tell Samantha tonight at dinner."

"I'll bring Moses and Buddy to visit."

Maggie stopped and faced him, suddenly very sure. "Bring them to stay, Joel. And bring your clothes. I don't want to ever spend a night without you again."

"I can see," he said, his neon eyes glittering, "that we aren't going to have time for a big wedding."

Maggie laughed. "No time at all."

As he wrapped her in his arms again, a hawk called in the clear blue sky. Maggie opened her eyes to watch it, feeling her heart soar in the endless depths of the sky. "I love you, Joel," she whispered, and laughed. "You, too, Mitchell Gray."

*   *   *   *   *

Silhouette Special Edition

COMING NEXT MONTH

#589 INTIMATE CIRCLE—Curtiss Ann Matlock
Their passion was forbidden, suspect . . . silenced by the specter of his late
brother—her husband. Could Rachel and Dallas reweave the angry,
fragmented Cordell and Tyson clans into a warming circle of love?

#590 CLOSE RANGE—Elizabeth Bevarly
Tough, disillusioned P.I. Mick Dante had long admired ethereal neighbor
Emily Thorne from afar. But when she approached him to track her
missing brother, temptation—and trouble!—zoomed into *very* close range.

#591 PLACES IN THE HEART—Andrea Edwards
When Matt finally came home, he discovered he'd relinquished far more
than he'd imagined. . . . But would Tessa make room in her heart for her
late husband, her sons, *and* the lover who'd once left her behind?

#592 FOREVER YOUNG—Elaine Lakso
Levelheaded Tess DeSain ran the family bakery—and her life—quietly,
sensibly. . . until flamboyant Ben Young barged into both, brazenly
enticing her to have her cake and eat it, too!

#593 KINDRED SPIRITS—Sarah Temple
Running from Ian Craddock's dangerously attractive intensity, Tara
Alladyce sought emotional sanctuary . . . in a phantom fling. But Ian
wasn't giving up easily—he'd brave man, beast *or* spirit to win her back!

#594 SUDDENLY, PARADISE—Jennifer West
Nomadic Annie Adderly kept her tragic past a secret . . . and kept running.
Then incisive, sensual detective Chris Farrentino began penetrating her
cover, pressing for clues, probing altogether too deeply. . . .

AVAILABLE THIS MONTH:

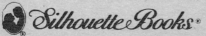

**A celebration of motherhood by three of
your favorite authors!**

Birds Bees and Babies

JENNIFER GREENE
KAREN KEAST
EMILIE RICHARDS

This May, expect something wonderful from
Silhouette Books — BIRDS, BEES AND BABIES —
a collection of three heartwarming stories bundled
into one very special book.

It's a lullaby of love . . . dedicated to the romance
of motherhood.

Look for BIRDS, BEES AND BABIES in May at
your favorite retail outlet.